THE SONG OF SYNTH

Also by Seb Doubinsky

White City
Goodbye Babylon
Mothballs: Quantum Poems
Zen and the Art of Poetry Maintenance
Spontaneous Combustions

THE SONG OF SYNTH

SEB DOUBINSKY

TALOS

New York

Talos Press books may be purchased in bulk at special discounts for sales promotion, corporate gifts, fund-raising, or educational purposes. Special editions can also be created to specifications. For details, contact the Special Sales Department, Talos Press, 307 West 36th Street, 11th Floor, New York, NY 10018 or info@skyhorsepublishing.com.

Talos Press® is a registered trademark of Skyhorse Publishing, Inc. ®, a Delaware corporation.

Visit our website at www.talospress.com.

10 9 8 7 6 5 4 3 2 1

Library of Congress Cataloging-in-Publication Data is available on file.

ISBN: 978-1-940456-25-6
Ebook ISBN: 978-1-940456-30-0

Cover design by Rain Saukas

Printed in the United States of America

To my friends Tabish Khair, Kris Saknussemm,
Matt Bialer and Matt Gangi.

To my wife, Sofie, for her support and much needed irony.

To my children, Théodore and Selma, for interrupting me
exactly when I need to be.

Special thanks to Matt Gangi, for letting me use the song-titles
of his wonderful first album, "A," as chapter titles for
The Potemkin Overture.

1. THe POTEMKIN OVeRTURE

"a model of life is the reason why
we take steps close our eyes dances like a puppet
we take steps close our eyes dances like a puppet
hanging
waiting on the line"

Matt Gangi, *Waiting on the Line.*

one. SUBJECT POSITIONS

The list of proxies unrolled on the computer's 22" screen, bone white on navy blue. Markus Olsen liked his interfaces old-style. A conservative habit, to be noted. *The only one. I swear.* He sipped his cold coffee absent-mindedly. *Disgusting.* The golden wiring of Synth began to connect and unfold behind his eyes in fractal possibilities, but he stopped it. There were no particular mental associations or hallucinations he would pleasurably link with the word "disgusting." Maybe some people did. He was *sure* some people did. *Freaks.* His eyes focused on the screen and he put the polystyrene cup back on the desk. The last proxy was followed by an IP number, which he checked. It was a valid number. *Sucker.*

"Gotcha!" he said out loud in the emptiness of his office.

He forwarded the address to the Central Office. In movies, this would have been an exciting moment, with music, close-ups and vivid colors. Action. Sweat. Testosterone. Here, it was the banal conclusion of a banal chase after a banal medium-skilled hacker trying to earn fame by attacking the city's National Bank security systems. The joker was going to have someone knock at his door in about twelve minutes.

He remembered.

The door shook under the heavy kicks. Like in a movie. Karen hid in the bathroom in her underwear and tee. No bra. They had woken up half an hour ago. The watch still ticked beside his pillow. He thought "What the fuck, this is it." He ran from the bedroom to the dining-room and sat in front of his computer. Started re-formatting his hard drive knowing it was useless. The Force could retrieve anything. But it made him feel better. The thought of it. The fact they would have to work a little to earn their corporate bread. Time stood still in the tiny apartment he shared with beautiful Karen and the earth-shaped mole in the small of her back. Eleven months of happiness. And now... He heard the door splinter.

Bad vibes. Synth was fading, letting gloom set in. Same shit with all drugs, going down. Synth was no better. Was worse. You only knew it faded when it was already too late and couldn't stir the beast.

Thrown on the ground, he was about to be.

Dismounted like a rodeo rider.

Dumped by a disdainful girlfriend.

Fragments of the door flew into the tiny apartment and a mess of blue uniforms trampled into the small space, yelling unintelligible orders. A scream from Karen. Sheer terror. They found her in the bathroom. One officer was sitting on him now, telling him it was useless to resist.

"As if," he said.

A steel-capped boot broke his nose. Hadn't seen it coming. Heard Karen scream again and he fainted in a darkness smelling of his own blood.

THE SONG OF SYNTH

Synth was disappearing like a beautiful cloud chased by a cold wind. He knew the symptoms.

He felt the little cellophane bag and rolled the last two pellets between his fingers.

✳

Going down in the elevator, he saw his reflection in the corporate mirror. Images came in loops. Vertigo. Fear of heights. Free fall. Crashing. Sweat quicksilvered on his face. It was black. He tried to smile it off and proceeded to settle his necktie, his hands moist with sticky black goo.

✳

The subway was packed and Markus found himself crushed against the window opposite the sliding door. Ten years already. *Karen screaming in the bathroom.* The Potemkin Crew. The guys, the *compadres*, the friends. A strange feeling of old-fashioned nostalgia swept through his body. *Sehnsucht.* He recognized the first symptoms of Synth withdrawal. The melancholy. The regrets. The illusions of the past. Sentimentality. Self-pity. A longing for nineteenth century poetry.

The neons had taken on a bluish hue. His eyes filled with tears. He had to fight it, although he knew he had already lost. It was hard to be a willing victim, sometimes.

Markus got out at the next stop. He still had twelve to go until home, but he couldn't wait. He pushed backs and crushed feet as he made for the door. Gasped for air on the platform. The glimmering lights of a soda vending machine attracted his eyes. The prices were outrageous but he had no choice. Drop the coins in, grab the ice-cold can. A slow motion dream. Cheap effects but real. *I need to find a quiet place.* He stumbled up the stairs. The rumble of the city welcomed him. The scent of CO_2 was blessed. His eyes looked around. *A quiet place.* He saw a bench, next to a phone booth. His feet moved in that direction. The ghost of Synth was already sitting on the bench, waving to him. *Yes, you control me now, you bastard. But wait and see.*

Markus sat down and his fingers twisted the soda can's screw-top. Cars zoomed by, pedestrians walked and waited, stoplights switched. A symphony. He smiled. The colors were blinding. Synth would tone everything down. It always did.

He rolled the two last pills between his fingers in the pocket of his pants, enjoying the feeling through the cellophane bag. In a few minutes, he would break free from Synth and control it back. Power trip. Total.

Markus dropped the pellets in his open mouth, washing them away with a gulp of the expensive soda. Cars zoomed by, pedestrians walked and waited, stoplights switched. A quiet place. Ten to zero, backwards. *Place quiet a.* Like it should be. He began to relax. His eyes caught a poster for the upcoming election on a billboard on the opposite side of the avenue. A picture of Olsen, the prime minister and leader of the National-Liberal Party. They shared the same last name. *A coincidence?* Words from a song floated back. *I had to laugh.* He decided to be on a beach, with white sand, palm trees and a beautiful sky. And he was. The grumbling of the cars was replaced by the gentle splashing of the waves. Karen would join him soon. He shielded his eyes from the burning sun and looked around. There she was, beautiful in her black bikini. No, monokini.

Whatever he chose. The glory of Synth. Karen waved at him and he waved back. A quiet place. Her breasts were magnificent.

*

When Markus finally got up from the bench, he was feeling much better. He brushed sand from his pants, took a deep breath and looked around. He had set Synth on minimal and only the colors seemed more intense, more real in a Technicolor® kind of way. *Always a sucker for classics. Fucking nerd.* Sørensen's image flashed behind his eyes. You are on a mission from God and his pipe. But he was on another mission now. He had to locate Dr. Sojo before Synth escaped again and held him captive. The freedom of the Western World depended on Dr. Sojo now. He hailed a passing cab, turning it into a 1940 Chevrolet. Synth had class.

*

The cab driver let him off at the corner of Grundtvig and Laugesen, right in the middle of Sorgbjerg. It was the rundown kingdom of the NoCredits, full of social rejects, immigrants and whoever had been so unlucky as to run out of means to sustain their own living. Of course, Viborg City wasn't heartless—it cared for its needy and proclaimed it on every billboard and in every speech—so it gave those poor souls a minimum wage that kept their noses above the waterline—just. But of course all the ungrateful bastards and bitches dreamt of big cars and flat screens, so crime helped them achieve the comfort their monthly checks couldn't provide. And Synth was a great way to make a good tax-invisible stash.

That's why, like so many fellow Cash or Credit bourgeois citizens, Sorgbjerg had become familiar to him.

✳

When he finally located Dr. Sojo's massive silhouette sitting behind a polystyrened coffee at the Sorgbjerg Central Station cafeteria, he felt a shiver of relief. It had taken him almost three hours. One of the longest chases in Dr. Sojo's chase history. People thought, people believed, people didn't know. "At the Green café." "Behind Nielsen's appliance store." "At his apartment." Until someone thought they had seen him here. Well, fortunately, that someone was right. And here he was, the Wild Goose himself, warming up his big hands around a black coffee, really looking like a NoCred in his worn-out khaki parka.

Dr. Sojo lifted his eyes through the imitation tortoiseshell glasses and a smile parted his heavy beard.

"My favorite customer," he said, pointing to an empty chair.

Markus sat down, feeling the Synth stretch in him like a satisfied cat. No one knew where Dr. Sojo came from. Rumor was that he was an old military researcher gone bad. Others that he was fired from a private clinic for malpractice or addiction. Some said he wasn't a doctor at all, just a a quack. But whoever he was or wasn't, every Synth junkie knew his name.

"Wassup, doc?" Markus said, extending his hand.

Dr. Sojo's fingers were warm from the coffee cup. It wasn't even winter yet, but he dressed like an Eskimo. Actually, Dr. Sojo was always cold.

"Business, as usual."

The Doctor sipped his coffee and looked around, checking out the crowd.

"Your place or mine?"

Markus smiled at the usual joke.

"Yours, of course."

Dr. Sojo stood up, towering over the table like a sequoia tree, slapped his large thighs and snorted.

"Let's go," he said.

✳

Dr. Sojo's apartment was a crummy two-room NoCred place, crowded with bookshelves, weird art on the walls and an impressive vinyl punk rock collection. The kitchen was a mess, with a filled-up garbage can, a clogged sink in which pale gray water reflected the weak light-bulb, dirty paper plates and stained polystyrene cups heaped on the table. A smell of incense filled the visitor's nose as soon as he stepped in, acrid but not completely unpleasant. A large couch covered with a red and pink Indian rug occupied much of the sitting-room, with a small copper coffee-table and two leather-covered Arab stools. How the bedroom was arranged—hidden behind an Islamic Jihad flag used as a curtain—was a mystery to Markus.

"Take a seat," Dr. Sojo said, turning on his cranky old stereo and lowering the dusty pick-up onto a vinyl album.

Music crashed into the room and the Doctor turned it down.

"Had a party with a lady friend of mine yesterday," he explained. "Forgot to turn the volume back down afterwards."

17

Markus sat down on one of the comfortable Arab stools that sighed under his weight. With Synth he could turn this dump into an Oriental palace, if he wished, but the color enhancement worked just fine for now.

Dr. Sojo sat on the sofa without removing his parka.

"I read in the paper the other day that they found a spot in space where there isn't a single star," he said, unzipping the top of his coat.

"Gloomy," Markus said.

"Think so? I thought it was kind of cool. No stars, man. Think of that."

"Complete darkness. Gloomy."

"That's one way to look at it."

"What's your way?"

Dr. Sojo searched in his deep pocket and found a crumpled cigarette pack . Marcus accepted one and they sat silent for a few moments, enjoying cancer chemicals, abnormal children and a painful death.

"My way is that we don't know shit about nothing."

They laughed.

"What can I get you?" Dr. Sojo finally asked.

The ritual question. Two years they'd known each other. Synth turned Dr. Sojo into a younger version. Ritual question. Wonderful verbal key.

"The usual."

"Didn't you come two weeks ago?"

Markus nodded.

"Aren't you pushing the envelope, son?"

"What do you care? I've got the money. I'm still Cred."

Dr. Sojo frowned behind his thick glasses, and squeezed the tip of his nose between his thumb and index finger.

"I like our conversations. I would miss them if you were locked up at Kronborg."

Kronborg was the psychiatric hospital. Markus shrugged.

"It's my fucking brain. I can do what I want with it. Been under a lot of stress recently. Need the recreation."

Dr. Sojo killed the cigarette in the ashtray. The music was harmonic chaos in the background. Synth began to unfold the CBGB 1979. Markus stopped it, wanting to focus.

"Yes, but you're going where no brain has gone before."

"You're a fucking weird drug dealer, you know that?"

Dr. Sojo smiled and settled back on the couch.

"Yes, I know that. I'm just warning you, that's all. It's still a relatively new drug. All possible experiences have not been recorded."

"Like the big black hole in the sky."

"Like the big black hole in the sky."

Markus crushed his own cigarette.

"It's okay, man. I'm an astronaut. You got the stuff?"

"Sure."

✘

The subway doors closed and he sat in the near empty car. Rush hour had subsided. A quiet place. His fingers played with the cellophane package warming inside his pocket. 28 beads, normally a month. Now two weeks. Less if he could. If he dared. If he had the money. Synth sent him a row of random numbers. Yes, he could play the lottery. But would he still use Synth if he was Cash? The thought lingered, threatening. 28 beads, the rosary of addiction.

two. curTaINS

The apartment welcomed Markus like a dying widow. Synth turned it into a 60s Danish Design loft. Much better. Suited the loneliness. Dashing. Perfect. "Anyone for a gin and tonic?" The party was just wild, man. All these chicks with pointy chests. Dangerous bras. Tight pants showing panty lines. Rock 'n' roll full blast play loud recorded in stereo for your listening pleasure. A couple of guests hung around the buffet, smoking weed and chatting, plastic glass in hand. Plastic phantastic. The colored lights gave words strange shadows. Markus undressed, throwing his jacket, shirt and tie on the sofa. A girl giggled.

✗

Markus sat in front of his computer, naked. The anklet shone darkly on the white skin. The Synth party had been wild, although he couldn't remember things clearly. The apartment was still arranged in its 60s style, but the people had disappeared. Fine for now. He clicked on the mouse and his avatar took a few steps in *Erewhon*®, the cyberspace city where "everyone is free to develop in any way they choose."

The site had appeared a few years ago and had been an instant success, partly because it was free and partly because the media had immediately put their spotlights on it, anxious to promote something "extraordinary" in this very ordinary life.

Markus had been asked by the Viborg Security Center to monitor *Erewhon*® at first, just to check that everything was legit and then to protect it from hackers, pirates and desperados, because big corporations had sensed a profitable market and had moved in.

Only Cash and Credits were allowed. NoCreds couldn't log in. And Credits had to obtain their bank's permission in order to purchase. Nonetheless *Erewhon*® was a fantasy that relieved people of their daily problems. The site was divided into regions, from the normal shopping mall to the exclusive, restricted VIP areas.

The official purpose was fun and business, in equal measure. Unofficially, it was mainly business, of course.

The whole thing was like a gigantic carnival, with virtual identities. And you could do anything—fly, drive a racing car, flirt, sleep in a castle, join a virtual war. . . Some things were expensive, some things were free. Like in real life. Except that it wasn't. Maybe that was the ultimate thrill. A legal drug of sorts. Good, clean, fun.

Markus's avatar strolled the main plaza, which looked like Times Square, with its huge neon billboards and 3D advertisements. It was night now and there was a light drizzle. The time and weather were tuned to Viborg City.

He looked around. There were banks, were you could actually open accounts, a couple of energy company offices, numerous mobile phone stores, two movie theatres showing the latest blockbusters, four music stores, one bookstore, an army recruiting office—if you wanted to join in a war of your choice. The Crusades, the Seven Warring Kingdoms, Napoleon, World Wars One and Two, Korea, Vietnam, the Gulf Wars, the Southeast China Campaigns, they were all there.

He had tried the Napoleonic wars. The Egyptian Campaign. Impressive. He had been in the French artillery. A massacre, they had performed. Thrilling. Camels blown to pieces. Quite a show.

He had been killed very fast, though. Short lived fun.

Still, the uniforms had been fabulous. Not to mention the Pyramids and the Sphinx, in the distance.

When he finally spotted her, she was sitting on a bench, right by the entrance to the subway. The most beautiful cars passed her but she didn't seem to notice, although he did.

She had chosen an eighteenth century dress.

It almost matched his nineteenth century English naval officer suit.

She waved as she spotted him, but didn't stand up.

"Hello there, Gloria!" he said. "Wonderful weather tonight."

She smiled as he sat next to her.

"At least we can't feel the drops. That's a plus."

"That's *Erewhon*®."

He studied her face. She had cut her black hair short and her blue eyes wore no makeup. She looked strangely calm and beautiful.

Gloria. His only serious flirt in five years. Only virtual, of course, but it made things easier. The masks were a protection against lies. The avoidance of eye contact. The queasiness in the bottom of the stomach. The phone numbers erased in the contact list. What do you do for a living? Are you Cash or Credit? Do you love children? Nothing like that with Gloria. She was a wonderful reminder of his loneliness. He had often asked Synth to recreate her in various erotic fantasies. Her avatar had the perfect body. Neither too fat or too thin. It was very realistic actually, quite different from most of the Barbie dolls you could see strolling around. He had himself chosen a Mulatto avatar, with green eyes. *Why?* Why not? She had never commented on that. And why should she? She was Gloria. She didn't care. That's why he liked her.

They sat next to each other, in silence, their shoulders slightly touching. Thanks to Synth he could feel her warmth through the fabric.

If I could only read thoughts. With Synth, maybe. He tried. Saw only code lines. Jumbled. Meaningless, like a madman's alphabet.

"So," he finally said. "What do you want to do? A movie? They're showing *Elric* at the Kino."

From the way she shook her head, Markus knew something was wrong. She wasn't the usual Gloria, although he was his usual sorry self.

"We won't be seeing each other any more, Orlando."

The news took time to connect, because Synth was screening for bad emotions. Suddenly he could feel the heavy cold raindrops on his shoulders. Suddenly he remembered he was sitting naked in front of his computer.

"How do you mean?" he asked, looking at her sad face.

"I'm getting married," she said, not looking at him.

Synth scrambled to protect him. Markus denied.

"It doesn't make sense," he said, as much to himself as to her.

She didn't move, didn't look at him.

Markus was really freezing now.

"Why?" he finally asked, feeling stupid.

"My fiancé—he wants me all to himself. I told him about this place, about you. It wasn't a good idea."

"This sounds like the start of a nineteenth century melodrama, Gloria."

She didn't answer, instead her pixels floated around as if propelled by a strange wind.

"I'm going to miss our conversations," he said, thinking he would be missing much more than that.

"I don't want to stop coming here, but I have to. I have no choice. Maybe after the marriage and all, I can come back. Maybe he'll understand. But he's very conservative. You know the type."

Markus didn't, but nodded all the same.

The whole situation seemed completely ridiculous—two cartoon characters saying goodbye to each other—but it hurt all the same. He remembered all the good times their avatars had shared and Synth began to overlay memories like in a beautiful film. The conversations. The movies. The walks in *Erewhon®*'s parks and open spaces. It was corny, but right now corniness was perfect. A refuge. A good way to keep from crying like a moron.

Gloria stood up and abruptly disappeared. It was the first time she had ever left without a goodbye, a kiss or a wave of the hand. Markus stared at the depressingly real emptiness of the virtual bench.

✳

The night welcomed him again. It wasn't surprised. It was accustomed to his routines by now.

I must find a refuge. My heart needs a golden cradle. Its crown has been tipped and I need to repair my orb.

Alcohol whispered through the neon signs. Familiar notes, like a distant melody, a flute in the mountains. He couldn't stay home. He hadn't felt so alone in a long, long time. In a country far, far away. Synth produced mirages of distant cities. Markus wanted sunshine. He got Samarqand, with its beautiful golden walls. The vision was so striking he had to stop and contemplate the majestic glass buildings reflecting the sun in every direction.

Samarqand.

The Evil Empire, along with Ur, Persepolis, Palenque and Shanghai City.

He wondered why Synth had chosen Samarqand for him. It came from deep down inside him, no doubt. Subconscious fears and desires, all rolled into one. Perfect image. Or was it a metaphor? With Synth it was impossible to know. Always the obscure poet.

Samarqand.

He stayed a while longer, trying to think what he would have done if this hadn't been a mirage. Walked into the city, visited the famous Temudjin mausoleum, drank mint tea. A subtle warm and sweet taste filled his mouth, drowning his tongue in saliva.

Tourism.

Not for him, any more. The ankle bracelet weighed nothing but pressed down his life like a sixteen ton safe. Mobility: the radius of Viborg City. Period.

What period?

What period would you like to live in?

Synth, the eternal joker.

Markus stopped at the corner of Himmerlandsgade. Gloria's virtual face continued to haunt him. In love with an avatar. How ridiculous. But the last ten years had been tough, emotionally. Karen had never contacted him and he had been unable to locate her.

Markus quickly realized it was hard to date wearing a security anklet. Most girls distrusted him immediately, especially when he wouldn't tell them why he was wearing it. He couldn't. He had signed papers. Couldn't disclose his job either. Otherwise, he would go back to jail for life. That was what you got for hacking into military satellites. Especially during a war. He was lucky not to have been condemned to death. That's what his lawyer had told him, after the trial. Markus hadn't thought about that. And he was sure neither Ole or Nick had. Youth. Bad craziness. Idiocy. Politics. Blindfold.

Metal Thunder Operation.

Hacking into war satellites, to render them useless.

It made the Potemkin Crew famous overnight.

It was also the beginning of their hell. The five satellites had self-destructed. Billions of dollars vaporized. Man-made supernova. Synth stirred at the reference, illuminating the sky.

He still didn't know how the police had tracked him down. *Karen screaming in the bathroom.* It had only taken them a few days. . .

Then they'd had their psychological fun with him and when they told him Karen would get the same treatment, as an "accessory to plotting against the state," he had given the others' names. As simple as that.

An accessory. Indeed. She hated computers. She considered them socially dangerous and emotionally disturbing. Her father had been a programmer for some high-tech corporation. A cold, distant man who only warmed up when he talked about zeroes and ones. Never a kiss or a hug. Only his back visible in his study, his back turned on his wife and daughter, his face eaten by the screen. His death was a relief. Stupid aneurism of the brain. Of course? Of course. Wires of the body gone bad. Karen's mother put the computer into the garbage can, to the dismay of the corporation. Apparently he had been working on ground-breaking projects and they wanted the hard-disk. They even offered money. Her mother told them to go to hell or go search the city's garbage dump. Ground-breaking, maybe. Heart-breaking, that was for sure. So Karen hated computers. But she loved him anyway. And he'd put her through this ordeal—because of computers. Again.

Now he was free—working for Sørensen under an assumed name—and the others were in jail for the next thirty years.

A traitor, just like in any classic story.

Congratulations, you've been added as a character.

Markus closed his eyes in self-disgust and shivered in the cold night. He buried his hands in the pockets of his vest, opened his eyes again and moved on. Neon billboards decorated the streets, announcing Christmas. Viborg City would thrive soon, all wrapped up in shimmering paper.

Another reason to feel lonely.

He remembered why he was out. Depression. *Looking for a friend in this indifferent city.* He thought about Dr. Sojo, but he'd already seen him today and he didn't want to make the man suspicious. He knew how paranoid Dr. Sojo was—and with reason. Markus thought about the pills hidden in a legit medicine bottle.

A friend. Could he be so desperate?

Yes.

Yes, he certainly could.

Then Synth helped him. It showed him a beautiful library, with hundreds of books crammed onto shelves. The sun shone through a glass roof, like a golden waterfall. The library looked ancient or middle European. Old men peered closely at titles—the leathery skin of their noses merging with leather spines—or leafed though books silently, half-hidden in the shadows.

That was why he loved Synth so much. It could really find the perfect image hidden deep in the subconscious and help you understand things from a different perspective.

Yes, books were definitely friends. Like music. But he needed the weight of a good book in his hands now. *Right now.* He wasn't far away from *Books and Wonders*, the cultural superstore, but he knew what downloads they had in stock. More precisely, he knew what they didn't have.

They only carried bestsellers and classics with the academic seal of approval, not *real* literature.

No freaky, accidental, strangely assembled narrations.

Only well groomed stories, to please the majority of readers.

Not the stuff he liked, in any case.

Viborg City cared for its citizens. They shouldn't read *n'importe quoi*.

Some days Markus was tempted to throw away his PersoReader—he hadn't downloaded a single good book in years. *Books and Wonders* and its rival, *Beautiful Pages* carried the same titles. Exactly. Democracy at its best. The only difference was the title being promoted that month.

The Academy of Writers thought it fair and their monthly checks and royalties supported that belief. After all, to become a life member of the Academy, you had to have sold at least ten thousand books—and ten thousand readers couldn't be wrong.

It was the same for music and art, with only subtle variations for their trades.

Viborg City was very proud of its commitment to supporting the arts. After all, in Babylon and Petersburg, artists starved. In Samarqand, they were killed, or so the media said—it was difficult to know the truth about the enemy.

Here they were published and protected.

Many writers and artists actually immigrated to Viborg City because of this situation. Little did they know about the inescapable "ten thousand readers" condition.

As a consequence just as many of them emigrated *from* Viborg City for the very same reason.

✳

The *Forgotten Shelf Bookstore* was empty, as usual. After all, it was only ten o'clock and most of the *aficionados* only came in after eleven. A strong smell of mint tea pervaded the shop. It reminded him of a Zoran Zivcovic novel. The place was a chaos of books piled up in apparent randomness, their dusty covers shining bleakly under a single 60 watt light bulb.

Real books.

Not digital downloads to your personal reader, with nothing tangible or real about them.

Not ten virtual pages generously given as bait, killing your eyes as you try to read.

No, genuine pages to actually skim through.

Amazing.

Markus heard a shuffling sound and Carlo, the owner, appeared from a back room, holding a steaming mug decorated with black and white photograph of a twenty year old Thomas Pynchon.

"Hello! What can I do for you today?" Carlo asked, blowing softly over the hot surface of his drink.

Carlo was a short and bulky man in his late forties, with a face that could be anything from Armenian to Italian, Jewish, Spanish, Portuguese or even Maltese—or a mixture of all the above. He never smiled, although his eyes did squint with glee once in a while. Tonight he wore a shapeless red sweater, large velveteen pants over torn slippers and he had covered his shaven head with a black, SAS commando woolen cap.

"Nothing much. I need a book."

"Don't we all? But so few know it."

"Anything you can recommend?"

Markus noticed a hardback standing like a roof on Carlo's desk, next to the credit card machine.

"What are you reading yourself?"

Carlo's eyes darted towards his desk and he sniffed noisily.

"A strange book. A novel sort of. Hard to figure out. *The Gardens of Babylon*. Published in Petersburg, illegal in Babylon. That's a first edition, signed of course."

"Would I like it?"

Carlo's eyes glared into his, squinting.

"You would love it. Or hate it. But it's expensive. And I haven't finished it yet."

"So that settles it, I guess?"

Carlo nodded and carefully placed his mug on a pile of books.

"What mood are you in?" he asked Markus, making his way carefully between the waist-high paperback skyscrapers that crowded the little shop.

"Heartbroken."

"Then it's either *Maggie Cassidy*, if you want to feel profoundly and intelligently miserable or *Quiet Days in Clichy* if you want to pull out of it."

Markus thought for a minute, letting Synth decide. The store turned into a Paris street, with cobblestones reflecting the sunshine. A woman was standing at the corner, clenching her coat around her in the cold April weather. Carlo was there, watching her while he opened his store.

Markus walked up to her.

She was not as young as he had first thought, her long face bore the marks of a hard life. Black half-circles shadowed her cheeks right under her beautiful brown eyes, making her cherry-red mouth look even more appealing. Her black hair was bobbed, and slightly disheveled, as if she had hurried out of her home.

"*C'est combien?*" he asked in French. How much?

She looked at him and flashed a weary smile. Her teeth were yellow, but regular and her breath smelled slightly of wine.

"*Cent francs la gâterie, deux cents francs le plat du jour.*" One hundred for a snack, two hundred for the whole dish.

Markus felt the bills in his pocket. Gloria's face hung in front of him like a ghost.

"I want to pull out of it," he told Carlo.

Carlo handed him the book.

three. REGIoN

Markus sat in his comfortable office-chair, gazing vacantly beyond the computer screen, his brain paralyzed with images.

Karen.

Memories came back like pictures falling out of frames. Why was he suddenly thinking of her? Why had she risen from the icy waters of the Styx like a resurrected Ophelia?

Karen screaming in the bathroom.

He'd tried to leave her out of the hacking operation, out of the Potemkin Crew's secret business. But she was his girlfriend, after all and, of course, she'd met Ole and Nick. She'd heard them conspire in half-voices. Hell, they shared a one bedroom flat! So sorry for her now. So sorry about the bathroom, the pain, all that.

He focused on the screen and the lists beside the keyboard. New assignments: Hacking suspects, credit card frauds, peer-to-peer site users. He had a dirty job to get done.

But Karen walked in and sat next to him.

"What are you doing?" she asked, sounding genuinely interested.

That was what was so great about her. Her interest.

She *had* loved him.

He looked at her and shrugged.

"Work."

That was what he had always answered.

"You don't want to elaborate?"

She was wearing a tight black t-shirt and white panties. Just like that day. He could see the fine hairs on her thighs shining under the neon light. She crossed her legs and leaned against him to look at the screen. Her body was warm and reassuring. They were in their old one-room, kitchen, shower-toilet, low-rent apartment. A feeling of security. He wondered for a second if Synth was building all this, then laughed.

Who else?

Karen put her hand on his shoulder, caressing him absent-mindedly.

"It's a list of numbers," she said. "With letters mixed in. Is it a program?"

Such familiar words.

She hated computers, but she loved him.

He nodded and shook his head.

"Sort of. It's a tracking program."

He looked at her. Her beautiful eyes widened in surprise.

"A tracking program? Who are you tracking?"

"A hacker."

The word had a metallic ring in his mouth. He noticed it as he spoke. Apparently, so had she.

"A hacker? I thought you were one yourself."

The office materialized briefly. He pushed Synth a little further and the old apartment surfaced again.

"Well, yes. *I was.* You know that now. But. . ."

She was still looking at him, her lips pursed, waiting for him to go on. Her heavy breasts fought against the black fabric of her t-shirt, he wanted to fondle them but the burning in his eyes made him stop. *No need to go insane. Not right now, anyway.* He knew what would happen with Synth if his mind strayed into erotic reverie. That was the curse of Synth: turning good things into unbearably good things.

"But what?"

Typical Karen. Would not let go.

"What?" she insisted.

There was a knock on the door and Markus jumped. He turned off Synth as much as he could and took a deep breath. The knocking resumed, louder this time.

"Yes, come in!"

A puzzled-looking security guard entered.

"Who were you talking to?"

"Talking?"

Markus tried his best laugh-it-off laugh.

"It was the Web radio. I was just singing along."

"Oh. Well, Sørensen wants to see you in his office. . ."

Markus nodded. He knew it was important because Sørensen had used the real voice channel, not the electronic one. Even at Viborg City Sec, wires had ears. So the personally spoken message was still the safest connection. The security guard left and Markus took the steel-cased elevator up to the 23rd floor. This time nobody walked in and no uncontrolled hallucination deranged his 8-second ride. Synth had left the building.

✱

"Who were you talking to?"

Karen, you moron. Who else? Yeah, who else? Catherine the Great? Show me Catherine the Great. Marilyn Monroe? Show me Marilyn Monroe. You fuck. You fucking fuck.

✱

"Who were you talking to?"

"Talking?"

Was he becoming insane? Markus remembered his conversation with Dr. Sojo. No one really knew what Synth was all about. It was so new, even though it had started a culture of its own. Music and art, mostly, but literature would come soon. If it ever got published. Synth worried the authorities. Especially its influence on music. So popular. There were Synth fuelled urban legends too. Like someone taking too much and becoming catatonic. Or murdering his girlfriend and eating her brains. Or even disappearing completely. Markus smiled. The last one would surely help.

He remembered his first encounter with Synth. He was at Carlo's, a few months ago, looking through the collection of Huxley, Burroughs, Moorcock, Ballard, Pynchon crammed on

36

the store's dark wooden shelves, all of them writers Markus had discovered in prison. The books were almost new when he had found them on the dull metal shelves of the library—probably too weird or difficult for most of the inmates. But this was precisely what had attracted him. There was something in the chaos of the words, in the torture of the sentences or the weirdness of the descriptions in these books that matched his own experience, although he had never done anything worse than smoking a lot of skunk and occasionally scoring a line or two from a generous friend.

Markus felt as if these writers were doing to literature what the Potemkin Crew had tried to do with the system. Change the lines of the code so that the code is rendered useless. Powerless. Harmless. It confirmed—albeit painfully—his commitment in his past actions, making him a much more conscious criminal than he had been at the time of the trial. He now discovered why prison turned criminals into hardened criminals: it gave them insight.

Markus was taking out *Cities of the Red Night* when he felt a presence behind him.

"Ah, I recommend that one," the large stranger said. "Just finished *The Place of Dead Roads*. Awesome."

The stranger was a giant dressed in a parka jacket, although it was the hottest June ever recorded in Viborg City. Conversation had ensued, then Dr. Sojo, as the stranger had introduced himself, asked him if he would like to experience some of the chemicals that inspired great literature. Markus thought about the anklet and prison. What would happen if Sørensen found out? What would happen if Markus kept waking up to the nightmare of inescapable reality?

Prison was inescapable reality.

Plain, solid horror.

Just like the time Markus returned to his cell after a walk to find his roommate beaten, lying in blood and vomit, his pants drawn to his ankles, red stains on his thighs The kid was eighteen and an idiot. Bragging all the time, showing muscle. Well someone had shown him *his* muscles. Markus pulled the kid's pants back up and wiped his puke and blood encrusted face and cradled him until the guards took him to the infirmary. He died there two days later, after swallowing a razorblade he'd managed to break into pieces.

Inescapable reality.

Now, every day in his office, tracking his old self down, trying to forget about morals and politics. Trying to forget who he was working for. Trying to forget who he really was.

Reality?

He wanted out.

He had bought the book and followed Dr. Sojo outside.

✽

Sørensen sat in his Nordic design leather and steel armchair and was lighting his pipe as Markus stepped into his office. The boss' face was hidden behind a blue smoke cloud and Markus thought about *The Wizard of Oz*. Synth provoked no reaction. It had dried up. The calm before the storm. In an hour or so there would be pain, anguish and sorrow.

"Olsen," the boss said in his gravelly smoker's voice. "Sit down."

Markus obeyed and accepted the genuine Cuban *cigarillo* Sørensen's manicured fingers held out to him and then the flame from a Silvermatch. The boss wore a gray three-piece suit today, making him look both terribly conservative and incredibly hip. His dark-gray hair was combed back and held with some dull wax.

"We have a problem."

Markus nodded. Why would he be here otherwise? He only hoped it wasn't with him. *Have they found out about my Synth habit?* An icy crown of sweat drenched his hair. If they had, they would have sent him back to jail immediately. Or to some psychiatric ward. Or that special hell of a psychiatric prison. They wouldn't give him a sermon and then arrest him. Would they?

"What kind of problem, sir?" Markus asked, savoring the delightful smoke from the cigarillo tickling the inside of his mouth.

"A security problem, what else?"

Sørensen's blue eyes looked at Markus as if he was tired of seeing him. Or maybe just seeing. His neutral face showed no sign of anguish, fear or emotion. *Power. Precisely. A metaphor.* Like Synth trying to get back at you the hard way.

"Yes, of course, what else?"

A puff of the pipe, time slowing down even more.

"Here, I've got something for you."

Sørensen handed him a plastic bag.

"Is it okay?" Markus asked, suddenly work-conscious. "I mean, with my bare hands?"

Sørensen nodded.

"Everything's been taken care of."

Markus fished out a PersoReader and a Viborg City National Bank CashCard.

"What's wrong with the card? Is it fake?"

Sørensen shifted his weight in the chair. He looked uneasy.

"I can't explain everything. You're not cleared for Purple. But you need to work, so I have to give you *some* useful information," he said, as if he was trying to explain something to satisfy himself. "We found those on the last hacker you tracked."

The door explodes and flies into the corridor.

"Take a look at the card. Do you see anything peculiar about it?"

Markus examined the plastic rectangle. It looked like a normal CashCard, gold colored and with all the numbers and digits in the right places, the chip glowing copper under the neon light.

"Apart from the fact that your hacker is Cash, no. And then again, there are so many Bourgeois kids who are dying for adventure. . . What's the catch?"

"It doesn't exist. It's not registered anywhere."

Markus exhaled noisily.

"Very nice forgery."

"Well, that's the problem," Sørensen said. "It's real."

Markus felt Synth buzzing in the background. *Not now.*

"Real? How can it be fake and real?"

"Well, the card might not *exist* technically, but it is funded."

Sørensen stopped, to give his words more effect.

"Billions."

Markus let that sink in for a few seconds.

"So where does the money come from? Where is it?"

"We don't know and we need to know. We found receipts at his apartment. Same card number. But when we checked the card with Viborg City National Bank, they denied its existence. There's no account attached to that card. Anywhere."

"How can that be?"

Sørensen stretched his lips into a forced smile.

"Exactly. We want you to find out how and trace the card back to its source. We are going to interview the hacker this afternoon. You'll come with us."

"Wait," Markus objected. "I'm not a. . ."

"You are a civil servant, paid by the Viborg City Security Department and you'll do exactly as you're told. This afternoon, at two p.m., information building, room 12. Clear?"

Markus nodded, then felt a chill run down his spine.

"I have nothing to do with this," he said.

"I know. You're the first one we checked."

"Of course."

"Of course."

Sørensen relit his pipe. His gestures were measured, as if he had an internal computer that regulated all his moves. Markus realized that it was raining. The drops slid on the window in long quicksilver trails.

"It's been ten years now," Sørensen said, his eyes half-closed as he sucked on his pipe. "Almost exactly. Next week, October 23rd. Food for thought. Happy anniversary, nonetheless. You were one of our greatest catches."

Markus regretted having killed the *cigarillo*. He could have used a blue cloud to hide behind.

"Happy anniversary to you too."

Karen screaming in the bathroom.

They'd dragged him downstairs first. He had not seen her until the trial. Ten months later. She was sitting in the middle of the crowd. She didn't even wave to him. Or wink. Or anything. There was just her face, among all the others.

Her face. Beautiful. She'd come once and never returned. He understood. At least, he thought he did. Later, Synth made things much easier. He *really* thought he did. The only question that had haunted him for the past ten years: *Did she know why she was free?*

Markus stood up to leave and Sørensen extended a hand. It was surprisingly warm and firm.

"Keep me informed."

"Yes, sir."

He reached the door then suddenly turned around.

"And what about the PersoReader?"

Sørensen smiled.

"I think you'll find his taste in literature extremely interesting."

✱

Back in his office, Markus turned on the PersoReader. It belonged to a Bjørn Christensen, who lived in the Nobel area, near the zoo—a fashionable place, full of neo-Bohemians, artists, crooks, wannabees, pretty girls and expensive cafés. A cliché in itself, every self-respecting city nourishes carefully to give the illusion of culture and modernity. All irony aside, he felt sorry for the poor dude and he carefully scrutinized the small picture displayed next to the address, as if he could get to know him better, but all he saw was a trendy-looking idiot, with a fashionable haircut and the usual look of disdain.

He went directly to the book section and checked the file. There was only one title listed. *The Potemkin Overture.* Markus frowned. He had never heard of the book before, which was

42

strange considering his dedication to the dailies' literary pages.

Still frowning, he began to read.

✳

Outside, it had started to rain. An icy drizzle prickled his face with a thousand frozen needles. Markus knew he was going to be late for the interrogation. The building was right in front of his own, a mere fifty meters away, a brick and steel-glass twin. They liked things to look alike in this country. That's why they were all blond, probably. Still he knew he was going to be late, and Sørensen wouldn't like that. He would say "you're late" and Markus would nod. Nothing more than that, and it would still be very unpleasant. Sørensen was unpleasantness personified. Probably got him the job too. Markus began to jog towards the revolving doors as the rain grew heavier.

✳

"You're late."

Markus nodded. Synth squirmed. Black sweat.

✳

Markus stepped into a steel gray cubicle, followed by Sørensen and a police officer. The facing wall was black, but he knew it was a one-way mirror—he had seen films. There was also a sound console, with two thin mikes attached, but no chair. Sørensen nodded to the officer, who stepped forward and

43

pressed a button. The mirror suddenly lit up, revealing a white room, with a man sitting on a chair. Alone. After a second glance, Markus noticed the man was in fact shackled to the chair, wrists and ankles locked in steel bracelets.

The prisoner was a young man, with longish hair and thick fashionable stubble. His eyes were blue and glassy. He wore the regular beige prison overalls, which looked like oversized pajamas. Markus noticed the beard was glistening on one side. The prisoner was drooling.

So you think you're so smart, hey boyo? You think you can press keys and change the world? You stupid university fuck. You know what you are now? You're no fucking hacker, asshole. You're a fucking traitor. A fucking traitor, that's what you are now, asshole.

Things had definitely changed since his arrest. No more good cop, bad cop. No more beating up with a telephone book. No more insults or threats. Just a chair, dead eyes and spit running from his mouth. Markus wondered if they had pumped him up with smack, turned him into a junkie so he would confess whatever they wanted him to confess. He had seen films.

Think you're so smart boyo?

Markus remembered the picture on the PersoReader. Rich kid. *2000 miles away from home.* Loose chords in the background. *Think you press keys?*

"Are you ready?" Sørensen asked.

Markus nodded, not really knowing what he was supposed to be ready for. Sørensen switched the sound-console on and spoke into the microphone.

"Mister Christensen, can you hear me?"

The prisoner lifted a heavy head. His eyes rolled slowly, but didn't seem to focus on anything.

"Yes," he moaned, as if the word was too big for his mouth.

"What's he on?" Markus asked Sørensen's back. "Did you give him heroin?"

Sørensen shook his head without looking at Markus.

"A new drug. Military. Ultimate truth serum. Apparently it works. Or so I've been told. First time we've tried it though. Consider yourself a lucky one. First-hand witness to the science of interrogation."

Traitor, you asshole.

As if on cue, two men join them, each displaying a small golden caduceus on the lapel of his tweed jacket. Both are carrying note-holders and a government issued pencil. One is an older version of the other, with white hair stretched back and yellowish skin. His colleague is a tall, bony man, wearing steel rimless glasses. His hair is short, blond and thinning on top. Not funny types.

"Surgeon-Colonel Andersen," said the older man, extending a hard hand. "My colleague, Lieutenant Böckel."

That was the extent of their presentation and explanation. Sørensen turned back to the microphone.

"Is Bjørn Christensen your real name?"

"Yes," the prisoner croaked, his eyes now staring at the floor. "I'm thirsty. I want to pee. I was born here. I am twenty-six. I don't really love my parents. My girlfriend's name is Emma. I. . ."

"Mr. Christensen?"

Sørensen's voice was both firm and cautious, making the ghost stare up. The two army quacks were taking notes, nodding once in a while, exchanging muffled opinions.

"Yes?"

"Did you try to hack into Viborg City National Bank's security systems?"

"Yes."

"Why?"

"I wanted to check something about the card."

"Did someone give you this card or did you design it yourself?"

"Someone."

"Who?"

"Jean Gray."

"Excuse me. Can you repeat what you just said?"

"Jean Gray."

There were a few seconds of confusion. Sørensen turned around once more. The two doctors shrugged in unison.

"You sure this works?" he asked them. "He's talking about a character from the X-Men comics now."

"It works," Surgeon-Colonel Andersen assured. "Up to now, information obtained with project 4B has been verified to be one hundred percent truthful. He's telling the truth, whatever the truth might be."

Fucking hacker asshole.

Sørensen furrowed his brow and shook his head.

"Yes, whatever. . . Mr. Christensen?"

"Yes?"

"Who is Jean Gray?"

"She's a member of the X-Men."

Sørensen shot a furious glance to the doctors who remained impassable.

"Where did you meet her?"

"Nowhere."

Sørensen let out a deep sigh and turned off the mike.

"Give me a good telephone book and some psychological leverage. . ."

He stared at Markus who felt his stomach turn. Yes, it had worked with him. *Karen screaming in the bathroom. You love her, don't you? Do you really want to send her behind bars for ten years? Ten years, think about that. Ten years surrounded by tattooed dykes who are going to turn her on to heroin and other pleasures. You love her, you fuck? You love her? Then spit it out. Spit it out.*

"Okay, we're going to try something else. Mr. Christensen?"

"Yes?"

"That book on your PersoReader, *The Potemkin Overture*, where did you download it?"

"Nowhere."

Markus felt the PersoReader in the inside pocket of his jacket. He had brought it with him although it was evidence. He wanted to finish reading it at home. He had to. It was about him. He was the hero. For once. No. Wrong. Not *for once*. Again. Yes, again.

You love her, you fuck.

four. GRoUND

The cold wind that rushed down the subway station stairs made Markus breathless and dizzy. He stopped at the top of the steps, letting his eyes take in the Sorgbjerg central square, with its medium height red brick buildings, its bleak neon signs and deserted streets. A typical November sight. The pavement glittered in the eerie half-darkness, in nuances of gray he hadn't known existed. Even the shadows breathed. Doctor Sax laughed in a corner. That was what literature was all about, right? Finding a name for every situation and impressing girls. Well, there sure weren't any girls to impress now.

Synth was leaving flashes of color and strange flares on his retina. He stopped at a lonesome hot-dog cart and quickly ate two hot-dogs; result—a queasy stomach and a parched mouth.

The vendor was a Samarqand immigrant, tired and dirty. Markus wondered if the food was poisoned. Too much TV propaganda. He directed his steps towards a familiar street, a familiar bar.

He stared at the prostitutes, grouped at the corner of Wiesenbergsgade, shouting at the occasional passing car, giggling and exchanging cigarettes. Most of them came from Samarqand or Timbuktu. Sad exoticism and yet he couldn't suppress a pang of desire. One of the girls looked at him and smiled. Her teeth were even and white, shining through the damp gloominess. He passed her, hesitated, then turned back.

✳

The hotel room was minuscule, but clean. Everything was clean in Viborg City. *Everybody is blond and everything is clean. Trademark.* The girl locked the door behind them. She looked at him, waiting.

An hour, he said.

She looked into her black and gold fake leather handbag and took out her CredMachine. He inserted his official blue CredCard and punched in his code. She showed him her work permit, with the last health inspection stamp. He nodded and watched her unzip her winter jacket. *Everything is legal as long as it is clean. Trademark. Blond everybody is.*

He began to undress too, sitting on the bed. He was about to take off his jeans when she wriggled her hips to get out of her black see-through panties.

"No," he said. "Come here."

She stepped towards him obediently, the dark bas-relief of her pubic hair just a few inches away from his nose.

"What's your name?" he asked, stroking her perfect hips, looking at her from underneath.

Clean and legal everything.

"Mardou," she said and he felt the last juices of Synth simultaneously short-circuit in his soul.

The Subterraneans. A book, he remembered. Sad-eyed Mardou. Kerouac's ghost. The smell of stale beer. Past things, broken. Karen screaming in the bathroom. Mardou. Good name. Good girl. Now, for the anesthesia of sex, I—

"Whaz yours?" she asked softly, stroking his hair hesitatingly and sounding like a good actress.

Her body next to his face attracted him like a furnace. He could smell the street, sweat and deodorant. He needed more Synth. This was too real. He pushed the girl gently back and fished for the pills in the pocket of his pants. He needed to regain control.

"Whazzis?" the girl asked, suddenly interested.

✱

He had regained control again. The room had turned into a luxurious bordello room of the thirties, with red draperies and a mirror on the ceiling—the latter being Synth's idea. They lay naked on the bed, sideways. His hand was caressing Mardou's beautiful ass, her smooth skin shining softly under the gaslights. He had no idea what her dreams were, but she seemed satisfied enough, her sad eyes looking through him and seeing whatever she wanted to see. His erection pressed against her stomach, warm and soft at the same time. *A blending of textures. Blood pulse.* His hands parted the cheeks slightly, and his index probed for the tight pink marvel. Mardou sighed and opened her thighs. They rolled on the enormous bed, she pinning him down by the wrists.

Her bush brushed against his penis. He closed his eyes. He felt her breasts stroke his own chest. She was playing with him. He enjoyed being played with.

She gently grabbed him and slid him inside. The warm moistness engulfed him like a burning chimney. Flames again. Burning him to ashes. *If only sex could make me forget.* He reopened his eyes. Pleasure overwhelmed him. Mardou kept sliding up and down his shaft, her stomach contracting and loosening up as she moved. *Belly dancer. Arabian nights. Golden sweat. Taste of metal inside my mouth.*

He felt his sperm boiling up inside his balls. He didn't want to come now. Too fast. Too easy. He hadn't even *tried* to forget. *Visualize the anklet. Karen screaming in the bathroom. Only sex you forget.*

"Oh," Mardou said.

It was like a whisper and he felt his dick exploding in her as she kept grinding her cunt against his pelvis, again and again.

"Oh, oh, oh," she said.

"Mardou," he panted. "Mardou, Mardou. . ."

She fell on him, all sweat and warm skin.

"My name is not Mah'dou," she said, reaching across him for a cigarette.

✳

Markus stepped inside the *Gustav Wasa* with its familiar half-light and retro decor. The bar hadn't changed its tacky, lower middle-class interior in the last thirty years, making it hideous, attractive and timeless. He looked around to see if there was anybody he knew, but the place was filled only by the vintage jukebox and the usual drunks scattered around, their eyes buried in the snowy white foam of their beer.

Markus walked to the large O-shaped counter and waited in front of the draft ale pump. He needed to collect himself in front of a beer or two and to lose himself in small talk with superficial half strangers. Maybe Dr. Sojo would show up—Markus had met him here a couple of times.

The waitress, a beautiful girl in her twenties looking extremely bored or tired, took his order and poured him a pint of Carlsberg. The PersoReader was still in the inside pocket of his jacket and he was about to pull it out when a heavy hand fell on his shoulder. Startled, he turned to discover Dr. Sojo, grinning his toothy grin, accompanied by a young man in an expensive Italian suit.

"Markus, Wayne. Wayne, Markus."

Wayne grunted something Markus didn't understand. He seemed drunk or under the influence or both. Perhaps Dr. Sojo had sold him Synth, although he didn't look like a Synth user. Synth was hip, this cat was Squaresville Inc. Wayne looked around, a half-smile on his nice face. Dark haired, with deep brown eyes, he was quite handsome and Markus noted with some jealousy that he had attracted the waitress's attention. Her bored expression was gone, she was smiling as she floated towards them.

"Wayne's not from here," Dr. Sojo explained. "He's from New Babylon. He's on a business trip."

"With you?"

Markus was surprised. He hadn't imagined the people doing *business* with Dr. Sojo looking like Wayne. Dr. Sojo laughed as Wayne ordered a round. The waitress looked enchanted to serve him.

"No, with the Viborg City National Bank. He got bored and a friend of his recommended me. Needed some thought material."

"What's your trade?" Wayne asked Markus, handing him another pint, which Markus placed next to his half-finished one.

"I.T.," he said, wanting to remain vague.

"I.T.?"

Wayne shook his head.

"Big crash in the next five years. Saturated market and technology expanding too fast for absorption. Drop programming. Invest in hardware. Do you have a girlfriend?"

"No."

"I have, but she's far away. In Marseille. Have you ever been there?"

Markus shook his head.

"Nice city. Lots of Arabs. I need to pee. Excuse me."

Markus watched Wayne wander off to the men's room and turned to Dr. Sojo, who was sipping his beer and looking amused.

"Is he always like this?"

Dr. Sojo shrugged.

"Dunno. First time I've met him. He's funny, though."

"Sure."

"How are you doing?" Dr. Sojo asked.

"How do you mean?

Dr. Sojo flashed a professional smile.

"You know. Being an astronaut and all that."

Synth suddenly triggered the brightest supernova ever and Markus had to shield his eyes for a few seconds.

"Good, I guess. The envelope is holding. A few slips once in a while, but it makes it all the more interesting."

Another nebula formed.

"Slips? Like in 'Houston we have a problem' slips?"

Markus shrugged, floating by in his space suit, the Earth glowing behind the spaceship like a blue sun.

"Yeah."

Dr. Sojo leaned forward, both elbows resting on the bar.

"Tell me, I'm interested."

"Well, it's like there's a hallucination leakage once in a while. Mingling with reality, without me controlling it."

"Wow," Dr. Sojo whispered, visibly impressed.

"Yeah. Wow."

They raised their glasses and toasted. Dr. Sojo suddenly winked at him and Markus turned around.

"I'm back," Wayne said, stating the obvious. "This place is dead. Do you know of any fun places?"

"Like where you can dance?" Markus asked.

"Like where you can watch other people dance."

"I know Karl's," Dr. Sojo said.

"What is Karl's?" Wayne asked.

"A strip club, not far from here."

"Females are a good commodity, although, like cars, they tend to lose half their value as soon as you've bought them. But the risk is minimal. Safe interest rate."

"So, do you want to go to Karl's or not?" Markus asked impatiently.

"Sure," Wayne said. "Sure."

✳

If Wayne wanted company, his wish was fulfilled. Karl's was packed with the usual array of Cash and Cred students, intellectuals, wannabees and other scumbags, taking advantage of the NoCred prices and of their own economically strong position to fulfill their illusion of Bohemian life. Markus knew the type well. He had been one of them.

They were sitting at a table near the stage, where a beautiful blonde girl with a sharp mouth and angry eyes was doing a modern rendition of the classic 60s Go-Go style. The 60s were big now style-wise, as their 'good, clean, fun' cartoon-like images helped convey an idea of 'friendly consumerism.' Markus lit a cigarette and tried to relax in his chair, while his two associates ogled the girl's beautifully designed breasts.

Pictures of Mardou—or whatever her name was—kept sliding back and forth over the dancer's body, like a wild slide-show.

"Have you ever been to Corsica?" Wayne asked no one in particular, his voice muffled by the cheesy music.

Two bodies merged into one. Fragments swirling slowly like ice on the surface of a still river. *Fingers probing, invading holes.*

The salty taste of sweat. A faint smile. The bodies moving. His body too. His body, dragged in by the force of desire.

"Isabelle's best friend is Corsican. I think he's a terrorist. I don't mind. It helps my business. Supposed to be superb. More beautiful than Greece. Have you been to Greece?"

Only one body missing. Karen's. The figure in the carpet. What you forgot was never missed until it was suddenly pointed out. *Could he remember the smell of her sweat? Could he remember how tense her stomach was when he licked her? Could he remember the way she lifted her hips so that he could push deeper into her? Could he remember anything?*

"I have been to Athens once. Very polluted. I saw a junkie beaten to death by two policemen on Omonia. Very violent. But the Parthenon is beautiful. They also have one of the last anarchist terrorist groups. Risk investment recommended. In the top-ten, actually."

Anything at all?

✳

The night was cold and beautiful, the stars crowning the black sky like a hierophant. It all hung like a beautiful tapestry over the roofs of the Strindberg Residence, the housing complex where he lived. Red brick and white-framed windows, five stories of pure Credit style, perfectly crafted to give the tenants the illusion of temporary comfort on their imaginary way up to Cash residences and summer houses. All power to the people. Yeah, he remembered. The old poster with the black fist up on Ole's door. Synth made a summersault within his soul.

The old fist up on black's door. Yeah, whatever. He was so drunk and high he had tunnel-vision. *Up on door.* Funkadelic seemed appropriate. Didn't have any of their albums though. Nick had them all—a complete fan. But Markus knew where to find some at this ungodly hour. The only place that never closed and where money was always welcome.

What is soul?
I don't know, huh!

✗

Lalalala, ladada
(x3)
Lalalala, ladada (ah, ah)
Lalalala, ladada

✗

So here he was again, cruising the cybernothingworld of *Erewhon®*, that so nicely brought peace to his soul with its commercial emptiness. He walked his avatar to the virtual *Yo Music* store, looking around for Gloria, with no real hope. Was she married now? Was she happy? He slapped his avatar's face. *What a fucking stupid question! What did happiness mean anyway? The measure by which every occidental life was measured. The impossible measure. Of course. One could never be happy. Well, not really anyway. Of course. Less sad, maybe. Less miserable at the max. But the lie, oh the lie. So perfect. So humiliating. Kept us spinning the wheel like stupid guinea pigs.* Synth tried to provide comfort, sending pictures of candy bars, hamburgers, tropical sunrises, female beach volleyball contests and beautiful Rolex watches.

The store was full of sexy avatars—teenagers having fun and pedophiles trying to find their prey, he guessed—did they know each avatar was encoded and therefore traceable?—did they know that Cyber Magic®, owner of the *Erewhon*® servers sold the code to companies so they could elaborate customer profiles and send them appropriate spam, ads and commercial trojans? The minute you pressed a *download* button in one of the two hundred virtual shops that existed there, you were caught in the net of the Net—freedom of choice, as they said—no more bad thoughts, mister Olsen—maybe there were tracking codes for those too.

He went to the virtual jukebox and looked for Funkadelic—but the first three albums were missing— actually they were there, but the link didn't function—just his luck. It was the same with books, he knew. He had tried downloading *Naked Lunch* a couple of times, but the link was dead. The message read "soon to be restored," but it hadn't been restored in two years—not enough readers probably, though *Mein Kampf* was available—he was tempted to add *of course.*

Markus sighed and logged off. No drug-induced Black Power funk tonight. If he wanted the music real bad he'd have to go back to Sorgbjerg and go to *Frank's Second-Hand CD Store.* Like Carlo, it was a goldmine for music lovers, at least for those who still had a CD player at home.

He got up and stretched. Bedtime. Synth would give him the most magnificent dreams. Something to look forward to. Flashes of Mardou and the stripper mixed. He felt a warmth grow in his underpants. Then he remembered the PersoReader in the pocket of his jacket. *The Potemkin Overture.* The novel about him and the Potemkin Crew.

He picked it up and turned off the lights in the dining-room. Time for a good bedtime story.

✳

It was really strange to picture himself, Nick and Ole as characters. Well, they all *had* been characters, in a way, especially during their *high treason* trial and the ensuing hype. He could remember the TV specials on them and the pile of lies or grossly distorted info that they were media-lynched with. In the City of Freedom, *bad guys* had to be *really bad guys*—evil sociopaths and the like. You had to be insane to rebel against this perfect model of a society. It was funny to think that the USSR had jailed its dissidents on precisely the same arguments. But politics were a thing of the past now. The anklet was all the politics he knew about and that was enough for now. Until Sørensen mentioned the past and Karen made her gigantic comeback in the forgotten cinema of his soul, in full Cinemascope® and Technicolor®.

He remembered

fumbling with the buttons of her shirt—a white cotton shirt revealing the white bra underneath—she stroking his hair and laughing—they were sitting on the sofa—was it her second visit or her third?—his fingers trying to hide their impatience while her breath crowned his forehead—his fingers moving slowly downwards—her shirt like a curtain opening on her lovely satin bra—his nose digging deep in her soft, perfumed flesh rippling with delicate laughter—she all the while not touching him, except for his hair in which her hands were buried—he kissing her while his hand made the great leap to her breast, finding its way beneath the cup, discovering her hardened nipple—the vertigo of the tongues, the slight change in breathing

she finally helping him out of his own shirt—still laughing as his head got entangled—sweet strangulation of love and desire—very Burroughsian to say the least—their stomachs touching and burning with that invisible fire

and he remembered the slow undressing and tongue licking biting kissing eating swallowing turning discovering while their bodies crashed into one another sweetly but fiercely in the fleshy walls of their soft machinery oh how he had longed for her for this moment oh how he had

her hand around his penis timid at first while he rubbed and rubbed where it feels oh so good yes yes yes and then her hand becoming more self assured and his own erection too tower of power rocket to the moon all that silly imagery that suddenly wasn't a metaphor anymore

but why think of poetry at a moment like this—kneeling between her knees in front of her dark forest—he noticed she had shaved the sides of her pubic hair—darker skin around the thighs like his cheeks at the end of the day—his nose discovering her real self first—through her bittersweet perfume—then his delicate fingers then his tongue—closing his eyes although he wanted to keep them open—but he was still shy in a way not for long but at that time yes—his tongue tickling and lapping and rolling and playing and tickling and lapping again—she not saying anything not even moaning as if her breath had frozen—only the movements of her belly going up and down like a fleshy wave—his hands on her hips feeling upwards and downwards—touching her like a blind man with his face buried deep against her

until she reached for his shoulders and made him join her kiss her fondle her some more taking his penis in her hand again and opening her thighs like a beautiful tree—the image had surprised him but that was the image he had the first time they made love—a beautiful tree

inside outside inside outside inside outside

the love dance

all the while Synth recreating it all in true-to-life rendition

he had looked directly into her eyes as he was coming shards of electric pain jolting though the small of his back

she caressed him sweetly afterwards like a child

he had dreamed this scene over and over in prison and Synth had helped him come in spite of the guilt

his naked penis squirting in the darkness of the cell without him touching it or anything—just like right now

amazing

yes, Synth was almost as amazing as love

and almost (almost)

just as good

five. REGIoN 2

In the emptiness of his office, Markus spun on his chair, the PersoReader between his hands, wondering who the hell could have written that book. Maybe Ole or Nick had managed to smuggle out a manuscript—although he had never imagined they had any special talent for writing—but to whom?

There was a publisher's name on the first page. *Worker's Books*. He'd looked them up and they didn't exist. Anywhere. He'd cross-checked with all possible databases—nothing. Markus sighed and scratched his head, putting the PersoReader down on his desk.

The name was a provocation.

He knew about provocation. *Agit-Prop*. He had been there. The Potemkin Crew proved it.

With the great results everyone knew about.

THE SONG OF SYNTH

He felt like a coffee and stood up to go to the vending-machine. He hadn't slept very well. Not surprising, considering he hadn't slept well in the last ten years. But tiredness hung over his shoulders today like a heavy blanket. Too many dreams about Karen. Visions, rather. Not vivid enough to be Synth creations, and buried too deep, as if he only saw—or felt—fragments floating on an opaque surface. Woke up many times, breathing hard.

Maybe another symptom of Synth letting go.

He thought he had been taking it regularly—how many since his last visit to Dr. Sojo? He had bought 24 and now he had. . . His fingers fished the cellophane bag from his pocket. 22 left. Impossible. He had taken one with Mardou and given her one. And then. . . He couldn't remember. But he hadn't taken only one—not for such a long trip. He had to ask Dr. Sojo if he'd given him some extra pills without telling him. He was his best customer after all. Good business move. Or maybe it was a new form of Synth. Stronger. Yeah, well, in any case 22 was good news.

But coffee was calling. He opened the door and went out.

The corridor was empty and all doors were closed. Kafka. To say the least. Orwell? Yes, Orwell. And Huxley for the drugs. If anybody wondered what literature was about, there it was, plain and simple: comforting references. You weren't completely alone in this world. The books whispered their words in your ear. The same with music. A tune for every move. And the links were never down.

✳

63

Markus had put the PersoReader aside and was now concentrating on the CashCard. Sørensen had been right. It *was* valid alright—it had a twenty-two billion account. He tried to find the algorithms linked with the pin-code, but there weren't any. Not in the conventional sense, anyway. He checked again. There were figures, but they didn't make sense. Nothing logical. Series of numbers and letters, changing every second or so. Alive?

The result was that the card didn't need a pin-code.

It wasn't protected.

You put the card into the machine and punched any number you wanted—it worked.

A skeleton key for cash.

Impossible. And yet. . .

Markus felt like the carpet was being softly pulled from under his feet. This was a new phase in hacking—if this was indeed hacking.

He suddenly wondered if Christensen was a spy on a mission from another city-state—Babylon, Petersburg or some other. Even Samarqand—rumor was that their technological capabilities were rising fast. But this fast?

An unprotected twenty-two billion CashCard.

Still, he had to start somewhere. Try to come up with something for Sørensen and his freedom. What would happen if he failed? Black sweat.

He looked for the account-number on the other side and punched it into his database.

Nothing.

Where in the hell did all that money come from?

He decided to let the matter rest for now and connected Christensen's hard disk. The Viborg City Security specialists had done a great job, recovering most of the data. He found the program Christensen had used to attack the central systems. Not very advanced—that's why he had been so easy to catch.

But something bugged Markus.

What was a mediocre hacker like Christensen doing with a novel you couldn't download from any existing site and a phantom CashCard so advanced it was absolutely untraceable?

Ghosts. He sighed and reclined in his chair. How could he fight ghosts? More important: did he want to fight ghosts?

He checked Christensen's Net favorites. Nothing interesting, apart from the usual Russian and Korean hacker sites. So he really was—or wanted to be—a hacker.

Sørensen had also given Markus the family background. A normal Cred family, with a father working in a furniture store and a mother employed as a nurse in the city hospital. A younger sister, still in high-school.

Synth suddenly sent Markus home—where he hadn't been since his parents had left the city, right after his sentencing. His father had been a professor of economics at Viborg university, his mother taught in a local high school. No siblings. Every hope concentrated on him. Of course, he had crushed those hopes. Now, once in a while, an email. They believed he was still in prison. For life. If only they knew—it might have crushed their hopes a little more. His parents were liberal-socialists. Believed in the goodness of mankind expressed in the free market. Markus had argued with his father so much about that, while his mother considered his radical choices a logical consequence of university.

"But Jens, remember our youth... We were quite red, also."

His mother, hair cut short, worried blue eyes, sitting at the other end of the Ikea wooden table. His father, balding, deep set eyes rolling upwards as he chews a piece of steak.

"I'm not red," Markus says. "I'm red and black."

"There you have it," his father says. "Red and black. Extremists. Tell me, what will you do when your revolution takes place? Shoot us?"

Markus shrugs and gulps some wine.

"Right now we are fighting against the war. Revolution can wait."

His father leans forward angrily, still chewing.

"This war is, unfortunately, necessary. South-East China is threatening the free world. It has to stop."

"The experts we sent still haven't found the super laser long-range cannon or whatever..."

"They will. You saw the satellite pictures. You can't defend South-East China."

"I'm not defending South-East China. I'm defending democracy."

His father laughs and his mother makes a disapproving clicking noise with her tongue. Markus can't tell if it is directed at him or at her husband.

"You're defending democracy by defending China?"

"No, all I'm saying is that we shouldn't have attacked first."

"And let them threaten us and world peace?"

"There are no proofs. And *we're* the ones threatening world peace right now."

THE SONG OF SYNTH
"Guess what I've baked for dessert. . ."

✷

After lunch at the cafeteria, he went back to his office and shut the door. He hadn't encountered anyone on the 14th floor in the last two days and he was beginning to think he might very well be the sole occupant. The last man on earth, still working for the Man. The irony made him smile.

The PersoReader and the CashCard were still on his desk, next to the flat screen. Familiar yet completely alien objects. What could he do? Trace, Sørensen had said. *Trace what?* Christensen hadn't confessed anything and he was the key, the answer. Maybe he didn't know himself. Maybe these things had been planted on him and they were trying to test their efficiency on Markus. Another conspiracy theory. A good one, at least. But too complex or evil to be true. One thing he had learned working for the Man these past ten years: the Man wasn't dumb, but he wasn't necessarily smart either.

He sat down at his desk, the half-empty polystyrene cup in hand. The problem here wasn't technical—well, wasn't *only* technical. It was a source problem. To identify, you had to know what you had to indentify. In this case, what? A book and a bank account. That was all and yet it seemed impossible for now, unless Christensen spat it out. He thought about telling Sørensen, then he remembered his comment about torture. Could they really do that to Christensen? There were international conventions and laws. . . Yet, everything had been suspended during the South-East China operations—another

67

reason for the Potemkin Crew to interfere—and nothing had been really clear since.

Christensen had done nothing terribly wrong yet—he had tried to break some security codes that would have led to other security codes, using tools that were desperately inadequate. It was the potential that scared Sørensen, summed up in the book and the CashCard. The potential and the unknown. How many books? How many cards? Where?

The invisible threat.

Ghosts.

The old primitive, irrational scare.

Using Markus the Ghost to track other ghosts.

Like Gloria.

Synth materialized her avatar and the familiar *Erewhon*® surroundings. She smiled at him as she used to, in her strange floating gestures. He sat next to her. Could he have been in love with her? Had she really meant so much to him? He tried to remember what she'd represented to him and thought he'd failed, until Synth recreated the exact sensation for him: comfort.

Yes, comfort.

The familiar silhouette waiting at the end of the day. The superficial chats with someone you could trust because there was no way she could ever know you and her eyes would never linger a few seconds too many on your anklet. . . His heart dried up and a feeling of emptiness invaded him, not unlike the symptoms of a Synth withdrawal.

Markus connected to the Cyber Magic® main server. He typed a few keys and was in after a couple of minutes. He hadn't unofficially hacked a site in ten years. He wondered if there would be a trace of his intrusion. He hoped not, otherwise who knows what could happen? A puff of the proverbial pipe and a trip back to prison. Fortunately, he had an alibi: the CashCard and the book. They gave him a palette of plausible explanations.

He typed 'Gloria' in the avatar list and found sixty-eight names and IP addresses. Fortunately, the picture of the avatar was shown next to the name. She was number thirty-four. Badia Khan. And she lived in the Strindberg Residence, a few doors away from him. His heart was beating fast as he scribbled down her address on a yellow Post-It®.

Finally, he knew what he was going to do after work.

✳

The subway car was almost empty for once, and Synth hummed nice electric songs for him as he tried to relax after his long and boring day.

His eyes lazily examined the stainless steel wall and found two political posters framed over the opposite window. He had forgotten that elections were coming up soon. Work and surviving his own shame had literally cut him off from everyday reality—and Synth didn't help, of course. One poster promoted the National-Liberals, in charge as he rode in the empty train, the other the Social-Liberals. Blue versus red. Symbolic colors of nothingness. He remembered his fights with his father. The Potemkin Crew believed you should burn all flags, including the black one. They had even put out a manifesto, some time before the Metal Thunder Operation. The leftists had screamed outrage. People needed symbols, it seemed.

"I am what you are not."
Big deal.
Was he becoming nihilistic?
Was Synth making him depressive?
Was it time for a holiday?

✳

Markus double-checked the address he had scribbled on the
Post-It®. It was fun to imagine he had probably crossed paths
with Gloria in the supermarket without realizing it. He pushed
the door open and as his shoe landed on the first step of the
concrete staircase, he suddenly wondered if she was ugly.

✳

Number 342. He knocked, as the doorbell hadn't worked.
No name on the door. His heart was beating. A romantic
moment no doubt. Somebody fumbled with the locks. Face
of a man in the opened door. Young, mid-twenties. White
t-shirt. Blond hair, of course. Handsome.
"Yes?"
Her fiancé? Husband? Brother?
"Er, does Badia Khan live here?"
The young man shook his head.
"No, she moved. Three days ago. We shared the apartment."
Like an elevator crashing to the ground, his heart dropped.
"Do you know where she went?"
Face shook his head again.

"No. Probably Sorgbjerg, since she couldn't pay the rent any more. She lost her job last month. She's a NoCred now. Shit happens."

A compassionate room-mate. Warmed the heart.

"Thanks."

"Sure. If you know anybody interested in sharing a flat, let me know, ok?"

Markus nodded.

✳

Sitting in front of his computer again, Markus wriggled on his chair. *Just a flirt, bitch. NoCred, man. Big time loser.* Should he? Could he? Hell yes? Hell yes.

✳

Ministry of Welfare and Social Crisis, List of Registered No Credits. There were seventy two Khan and eight had a first name starting with B. She was the seventh one. And she did live in Sorgbjerg now. Markus wrote down the address.

✳

Sorgbjerg central station stood around him like a cathedral. *Fire in the hole. Millennium. Black plague. Shell-shock.* Strange associations collided in his brain. Black sweat. Metal tasting tongue. *Crossfire. Heavy losses. Jerusalem.* Markus crossed the busy hall to the men's room. Terrible smell and blinding white light.

Hell? Already? The two sinks were taken and there was a short line in front of him. *Waiting on the line. Your country wants you. Allahu akbar.* Markus felt his veins turn to lead, his hand stuck deep inside his pocket, squeezing the cellophane package. It struck him he had at last become a junkie.

For real.

Hell? Already?

⁂

"No, man, these pills are the same as last time. No tampering, no new batch. The same. Exactly. Why?"

⁂

Dr. Sojo opened the door and let Markus in. A cloud of blue smoke pervaded the living-room, like a foggy morning.

"Don't tell me you need more," Dr. Sojo said, half jokingly.

Markus sat on one of the Arab stools. He wondered why he was here. Fear? Maybe. In a way. Somewhat.

"No, no, I still have plenty. Actually. . ."

"You know Wayne almost bought everything I had in stock? Man, he *loved* the stuff. Reminded me of you."

Dr. Sojo's eyes glimmered behind his glasses.

"Wayne?"

Dr. Sojo nodded.

"He was enthusiastic. Told me Synth is the greatest drug since LSD. That its popularity would grow exponentially. That I would become a millionaire. Actually, he might not be wrong. Have you seen today's paper?"

Markus shook his head.

"No, I've been somewhat. . . disconnected, the past few days."

They both grinned. Dr. Sojo pointed to the first page of *Aftenbladet* lying on the couch.

The new drug destroying our children, the headlines read.

With a black and white picture of junkies doing something.

"A revolution is on its way," Dr. Sojo said. "Nothing more dangerous than spoiled rich kids messing with mind-bending chemicals."

He laughed. Markus smiled politely. He knew that rich kids on dope were still rich kids. They would rebel, yes. A little. But not revolt. They had absolutely no reason to.

"So, what can I do for you?"

"Well, I need to know if the pills you gave me last time are different from the ones before?"

"No, man, these pills are the same as last time. No tampering, no new batch. The same. Exactly. Why?"

*

"Wow," Dr. Sojo said. "Wow, wow, wow. Twenty-four hours. That's a *long* trip. Be careful man. The Final Frontier, you know?"

Markus shrugged.

"The withdrawal was no worse than before. Actually, it felt shorter and milder. But that could also be a Synth thing."

Dr. Sojo agreed.

"Wow," he said again.

*

The Herman Bang Social Projects stood behind the station, four gray blocks with grayish-blue window-frames. At least the city wasn't lying about the bleakness of NoCreds' living conditions. Nothing like a straight stare in the eyes and a swift kick in the balls. Speaking of which. . . Was he ready? Was he not ready? How ready was he? His hands were buried deep in the pockets of his coat and his misty breath preceded him by a few inches. Stars turned overhead because they just had to. He stopped on the parking lot, hesitating.

All the windows of the five-storey building were lit, like a gigantic luminous chess-board. Synth began to move, but Markus stopped it. He wanted his corny metaphors to remain his own and he wanted to face Gloria/Badia as she was, not like some gigantic chess-queen or whatever.

He stood fretting, then moved on. His hand pushed the entrance door open and his eyes scrutinized the names on the mailboxes. *B. Khan*, fifth floor, 505. Finally, he had found her. *Good cop. Have a donut.*

A crown of sweat beaded his forehead. What would she say? What would her fiancé say? *Why am I here?* He didn't know, but it was as if a magnet pulled him up the stairs, slowly, steadily. She had been his only friend, that's why. His only flirt. His only *human* contact, although it had been virtual. The wonders of science. *Weird science.* He missed her already. He felt like an abandoned child looking for its mother. *I don't care if she's a prostitute. I don't care if she hates me. I don't care if she's butt-ugly. I want to meet her. I do, I do, I do.*

His body weighed a ton and grew heavier and heavier. Soon his feet would sink into the concrete steps and the stairs would collapse under his weight, burying him alive. A grave of gravel, concrete, rusted steel and piss yellow paint. How romantic.

✳

"Yes?"

Markus opened his mouth and closed it slowly. Things were never as one imagined them.

For instance, he imagined her fiancé opening the door, and all his own courage disappearing like dirty water down the drain, with white shaving foam and minute black hairs.

But—

✳

"Yes?"

Markus opened his mouth and closed it slowly.

The young woman standing in front of him in her tired training suit, a yogurt with the spoon sticking out in her left hand, was a normal woman. Thick black hair, black eyes, medium height, pretty, but not exceptional.

"Yes?" she asked again.

"Gloria?"

Markus' voice croaked, making him feel stupid.

The young woman frowned and took a step back, her eyebrows almost meeting over her small pointy nose.

"Who are you?"

"Orlando."

Gloria/Badia's face twisted slightly, as she tried to figure out what mask she should wear. A slight smile finally spread across her lips.

"You."

Markus nodded.

"Me."

She stood aside and gestured him in with the yogurt holding hand. The apartment was the typical NoCred crappy functional two rooms, with a tiny functional kitchen and, Markus imagined, a tiny functional bathroom. There were movie posters on the walls and a small bookshelf. Classics, he noted, with some distaste. The TV was on and there was a red couch to sit on. Markus hesitated.

"I'm not staying long. I just wanted to say 'congratulations.'"

Badia sat on the couch stirring her yogurt. On the table there was a plate with a few leaves of salad and a beer.

"Congratulations for what?"

Markus felt very warm and very stupid.

"Your marriage."

Her laughter hurt his ears. It was brief and as cutting as mirror shards.

"What marriage? There's no marriage. . . You can sit down, if you want. It's actually nice to put a face on you. What's your name by the way?"

"Markus. You're not getting married?"

He grabbed a folding chair and sat down, not daring to open his jacket although he found the heat almost unbearable. Synth offered the Arctic, which he declined.

Badia shook her head.

"No, no marriage. That was just a lame excuse to tell you I wouldn't be back in *Erewhon*® for a long time. Didn't want to tell you the truth, that I have been downgraded to NoCred. You understand, don't you?"

Markus looked around. Gloria's real face, her real apartment. He thought about their talks, their complicity, their affection, but the small TV screen seemed to attract his attention like a dark magnet.

"Yeah, I do. Well, I think I do. I'm Cred myself."

"So you understand. NoCred. The Black Hole. At least my debt isn't huge. Should be back up in a couple of years."

Markus nodded. That's what all NoCreds said. But he knew that once you were down, you couldn't come up. The City owned you—they said *helped you*—and very, very few NoCreds ever made it back to Cred. A bestselling biography now and then. A TV special. Hundreds of self-help books.

Their eyes met and she smiled again. She put the yogurt on the table and patted the sofa next to her.

Markus complied, feeling heavier and heavier. He suddenly wondered if he wasn't experiencing Synth withdrawal symptoms, but no. He was simply experiencing reality.

Their shoulders almost touched and Markus could smell her—sweat, perfume, deodorant and spicy food subtly mixed together.

"How did you find me?" she asked, her eyes on him as she rested her elbow on the back of the couch.

Markus realized he liked her face. She had strong cheekbones he hadn't noticed at first and her black eyes were intelligent, reinforcing the erotic harshness of her thin lips. He lied.

"I work for Cyber Magic®. Network maintenance. I got access to the customer list."

She nodded, apparently unmoved by the illegality of the process.

"Well," she said, "here I am. And here you are, Orlando. I mean. . . Markus. For real. Isn't that weird?"

Markus nervously fingered the buttons of his jacket. He was beginning to regret his mindless impulse.

"Yes, it is. It's my fault. It's stupid. I think I'd better go now."

Her hand caught his arm as he was about to rise from the couch.

"Are you in a hurry? You had plenty of time to talk in *Erewhon*®. Or is the NoCred situation bothering you?"

Markus sat down again. Synth was no help. Or he felt it was no help, controlling it firmly with his mental reins. His thoughts collided in endless colorful accidents.

"No, not at all. On both counts."

They smiled and there was a long pause. The TV screen flickered and mumbled to itself on the other side of the small room.

"I miss my computer," Badia finally said. "And my broadband connection. That's the worst part of being here. I'm stuck in the middle of reality and there's no way of escaping."

Markus thought about the Synth pills rolling around their cellophane wrap in the warmth of his pocket.

"My plan," she resumed, "is to save enough so I can get a second-hand computer and a broadband subscription. With my wages, I should be able to be back in *Erewhon*® in a year or so. I miss our talks. I really do."

"Me too."

They stared at each other, smiling. Markus enjoyed looking at her in a finer resolution than 1024 x 768.

Karen hated computers.

six. shIfT

Staring blankly at his office wall, he wondered how Ole and Nick were faring. After the trial, they had been sent to different prisons with a strict interdiction against getting in touch again. Markus didn't even know to which prisons they had been sent. The only thing he knew was that they had been sentenced to thirty years each—a shorter term than his own because they only had been *accessories* to the crime, which was true, in a sense. But—

They had been a team.

Real good friends.

Sharing politics, IT classes and booze. Youth. Ideals. Vomit. Dirt. Illusions. Anger. Rebellion. Lucidity.

Key words.

Satellites locking on.

No more viruses, though.

Youth of today lobotomized with comfort and the pursuit of happiness. Even the NoCreds - and that was the worst part of it all. No fear of the future. Slaves all their lives. Provided for as long as they provided back. Then medicated retirement homes. They could cast their votes there too. Special voting machines with large letters so that they could read out the names of the candidates.

Liberal-National or Social-Liberal?

Red or blue?

Zero or one?

Synth trembled and tried to escape, but Markus held it down with a tight fist. He had his own reality check with Badia last night.

He had found her face attractive. *Her high cheek bones and black eyes were intelligent, reinforcing the erotic harshness of her thin lips.*

She'd smiled and asked him if he wanted a beer.

"Sure."

They drank from the can. No glasses offered. None needed. They were old friends, after all. Three years of cyber talking. Now, without the avatars to protect from one another. Synth began to reconstruct *Erewhon*® and this time it was fine. The old bench. The cinema. The bookstores. She smiled. Synth hesitated. Gloria? Badia?

Badia.

He suddenly felt like kissing her, but the anklet tightened up.

"It's funny to see you for real," she said, running her hand through her hair. "You're not at all like I pictured you."

"I hope you're not too disappointed."

She shrugged and Markus felt a pinch in his heart.

"No. Surprised. Destabilized."

"Me too. Reality often has that effect on me."

They laughed.

For once, he had taken a cab home. Needed to feel the confusion and loss on a black leather back seat, the city turning in the rear window.

Synth slowly dissolved and the sharp light of the office hurt Markus' tired eyes.

Synth was digression.

Digression was life.

Yet the syllogism didn't have a third part. No *therefore*. Just a statement hanging in mid-air. Maybe he should quit Synth altogether. Maybe he should go back to facing the harsh reality and see what happened.

Actually, he realized, he had never done that.

Childhood had been childhood, and adolescence, well, a hormonal initiation novel. And youth—ah, youth. Illusions. Politics. Rebellion. Action.

For what?

Freedom.

Yes, freedom.

He was surprised to notice that Synth didn't react to the word.

Freedom.

Fantastic word meaning what? To be out of prison when in prison. But then, what else?

Was freedom a self-sufficient word, an empty shell in which one could cram whatever one wanted?

Freedom.

He tried to make Synth react, but only got black sweat and chills. Bad juju.

"Freedom," he insisted.

His head split in two and his own image stood in front of him, grinning stupidly. The worst possible toothache drilled his jaw and he couldn't repress a shrill yelp.

For Synth, it seemed that freedom was pain and bad craziness. Okay. He accepted that and returned to his computer screen. Better leave freedom aside now and concentrate on real issues, like NOT returning to prison.

We want reality and we want it now.

Synth produced a shopping mall, with the delicious smell of a first rate cafeteria.

✳

The door suddenly burst open and Markus nearly fell from his seat. It was Sørensen, looking very upset, with flushed cheeks and shiny eyes.

"Olsen, we have a problem. A very serious problem."

Markus was confused.

"Again?"

Sørensen shut the door carefully.

"What?" Markus asked again.

"Christensen. He's dead. Was killed, actually."

"When?"

"This morning, in the shower. His throat was slit."

"Who did it?"

Sørensen shrugged.

"Nobody. Everybody. We're putting all the prisoners in solitary."

"You know why he was killed?"

Sørensen's face distorted into a grimace.

"That is the question. Too early for a gang related action. Too early for him to have made enemies. What's more, he had an individual cell. So it's probably a hit."

Markus pondered this.

"The card? The PersoReader?"

Sørensen nodded.

"Of course. What else?"

Yes. What else? Black sweat.

"Terrorists," Sørensen mumbled, as if to himself.

"What, sir?"

"Terrorists. This is clearly linked to a major operation. Maybe they wanted to use the card to buy weapons. Nuclear waste, biological weapons. . . Maybe they already have. The clock is ticking, Olsen. Everything is in your hands now."

Sørensen wiped his forehead with a Kleenex. Markus wondered if he was on drugs too. Amphetamines.

"Yes, sir."

"Good, good. Keep me informed."

The door slammed.

Amphetamines?

✳

Panic, anyone?

Synth produced a woody vale on the flank of a formidable mountain. Something moved between the trees, like a

83

three-dimensioned shadow and a creepy scream suddenly filled Markus' ears, making him want to turn and run away.

The Great God Pan.

Horns, hooves and flute.

But Markus didn't turn and run. He remained, staring at the edge of the forest.

He wasn't panicked.

Not in the least.

With a shrug, he dismissed the hallucination.

What was he, then?

Amused. That was it. Amused at the irony of it all.

✳

Badia's body was fantastic. He couldn't believe he was against her, naked, on the sofa. They hadn't turned the TV off and it was still projecting programs and ads onto their moving flesh. Her breasts were soft under his hands, only the nipples hard and willing. Her back, a long curve. The angle of her hips, perfect against his. They weren't machines, programs, citizens. They were naked and making love. Her eyes were closed as if she was drowning—drowned?—and he, the swimmer, was slowly taking her back to the surface with kisses and thrusts. She hadn't minded the anklet when he'd shyly shown it to her before removing his trousers.

"What did you do?" she'd asked. "I hope it wasn't violent."

He'd shaken his head.

"It wasn't violent, I swear."

Just destroyed a satellite. Nothing much, really.

"Then I don't care."

She opened her eyes and smiled as he moved inside her, along her warmth and welcoming moistness. She was real. She was here. She was Gloria. No, she was Badia.

She was both.

Synth flickered and hesitated.

Later, in the back of the cab, he wondered if it really happened or if it was yet another of Synth's tricks. The feeling of loss and loneliness. Where did that come from?

✷

The irony of it all.

✷

After work, he felt like seeing Badia again, but he hesitated, standing with his cell phone opened at the foot of the Viborg Security building.

The evening sky was wet and gray, darkening on the eastern edge. Markus stared at the large billboard standing over the square. "Vote Olsen." The prime minister, wearing a white shirt with no jacket and tie, was smiling. A Liberal-National trying to pass for a Social-Liberal. It had worked until then. It was his third election. Ten years since his first. Potemkin Crew anniversary, exactly. The elections. Tomorrow. Yes. He had forgotten.

"What's the matter, son? Don't you believe in democracy anymore? Are you becoming a fascist? Worse even, a nihilist?"

85

He shut the phone and walked to the subway station.
"*Are you becoming, son?*"

✳

Viborg City, pearl of the North, throbbed overhead, with its copper roofs, second-hand bicycles and wide canals. Tourist attractions. The Hamsun Wheel. Nordic gardens. Nougat ice-cream. Beautiful women. Chilled beer. A catalog of colorful pages. A dream within reach. Markus smiled and looked at his ghost reflected in the black window-pane, trembling in the thundering chaos of the train's wheels. He looked tired. He looked absent. He looked.

✳

Erewhon® was its usual self, filled with avatars and on-line shops. Only Gloria was missing and that felt like a huge black hole in the scenery. To experience melancholy in cyberspace was one of the strangest feelings Markus ever had. Synth offered Caspar Friedrich, a yellow moon shining over dramatic clouds. Perfect. It matched his avatar's 19th century British Navy uniform. The streets were half-empty, indicating either a temporary loss of interest among the general public or a football match on television involving the national team.

Markus strolled slowly along the deserted shops, answering politely when spoken to by unknown avatars. Without Gloria though, the emptiness and shallowness of this recreation struck him painfully.

A paradox.

Emptiness making emptiness palatable.

He arrived at the usual bench—unoccupied now—and sat down.

"Worse even, son?"

Gloria.

Had he fucked her or—?

Who?

Badia?

Her body rubbed against his, her nipples rolling hard as small thumbs up and down his chest. Synth could be so real sometimes. But it had been real, hadn't it? Impossible to remember. No, incorrect. Impossible to tell if the memory was real or imaginary.

Black sweat.

He turned away from the computer screen and stood up. Drowning with eyes wide open. He stretched and extended his hands to feel the emptiness. Synth was the only reality now, or so it seemed. He took out his cell phone and rang Badia. A voice told him the number wasn't registered. That topped it. He couldn't suppress a bitter smile. Had she given him a wrong number on purpose, or had he punched it in wrong as she had enumerated it to him? He tried to collect his thoughts, but only a blurred chaos came across. Was it Synth? Was it the alcohol? Was it old age?

Another thought crossed his mind.

Christensen. Dead. Throat slit, throwing up blood.

The CashCard. Limitless money. The end of the rainbow.

The PersoReader and the unknown novel. A best-seller. He, the hero. Ha, Ha.

The Potemkin Crew's tenth anniversary. Something he should have forgotten. Something he should have. Something.

But couldn't.

Wouldn't.

Couldn't.

Maybe Synth wanted him to concentrate on the case and forget about Eros and Agape.

Maybe Synth was Sørensen in disguise.

Something moved awkwardly inside him, making him feel sick. Black sweat. *I shall not think bad thoughts. I shall not think bad thoughts.* Synth was freedom. Synth was good.

GOOD.

Images of suntanned, bikini-clad girls playing beach-volleyball surrounded him.

*

Markus was relieved to see that Carlo's bookstore was empty as he stepped in. Some Synth-Jazz played in the background, its twisted melody accompanying a cloud of smoke rising from behind a pile of books.

Carlo was sitting at his desk, reading a worn-out vintage paperback. A hand-rolled cigarette. He waved when he noticed Markus, but didn't put the book down.

"So, finished the Miller? How's the heartache?"

"Gone. Now, it's more of a headache."

Carlo frowned.

"Don't think I've got anything for that. On the contrary."

Markus smiled.

"Maybe not."

Carlo stared quizzically at the PersoReader Markus had produced.

"You know I don't do downloaded books."

"I know. But this one is special. You might find it interesting."

Carlo looked at the screen and stared back at Markus.

"Yes? What's the problem?"

"The problem is that this book is not registered anywhere and the publishing company doesn't even exist!"

Carlo's lips extended and he laughed.

"Man, where have you been all your life? In prison?"

The joke slid on Markus like a chilled blade.

"What do you mean?"

"I mean that everybody knows—well, almost everybody, it seems—about *Workers' Books*! They also have *Workers' Records*, *Workers' Films*, *Workers' Art* and maybe even more. . ."

Markus suddenly felt both dizzy and ridiculous.

"How come I can't find them anywhere?"

"Because you need to go to their website. Actually, even if I only sell permanent books, I do download some of their fiction, once in a while. Very good, generally. I heard it's the same with their music. And they have huge archives where you can find facsimiles of rare and out-of-print books. . . And free too. Amazing."

Carlo was getting excited as he spoke and his cigarette danced on his lower lip like a tiny newspaper sheet in the wind.

"Actually, what you have here is the first novel they published, when they started some years ago," he resumed, tapping the PersoReader screen with a strong finger. "A world-wide success. Too bad it's free—the author could've made a fortune. Bestseller, if ever there was."

Markus' mouth was dry.

"How come I've never heard of it?"

"Because you're too square, my friend, that's why."

The shop door opened and a massive silhouette made its way through the piles of books like a grizzly bear in a forest.

"Hello there, ladies and gentlemen," Dr. Sojo said, waving a huge paw. "Hope I'm interrupting something."

"Absolutely," Carlo said, crushing the already extinct cigarette into a full ashtray. "This gentleman never heard of *Workers' Books* and everything that goes with it."

Dr. Sojo stared at Markus with undisguised surprise.

"Never hear of *Nowhere*? *You*?"

"Never heard of what?"

He remembered Christensen.

"*Nowhere*."

Dr. Sojo and Carlo exchanged a long glance.

"Should we tell him or should he beg?" Dr. Sojo asked.

"I think he should beg," Carlo said.

"An astronaut like you," Dr. Sojo added, clicking his tongue. "Anyway, as you are one of my privileged customers, I shall fill you in. *Nowhere*, actually spelled *KnowWhere*, is a secret virtual world, the paradise of hackers, artists and con-artists. . ."

Carlo nodded and began to roll another cigarette.

"By the way doc, sorry to interrupt, but do you have my mail?" Carlo interjected, eyes focused on tobacco and rolling-paper.

Dr. Sojo nodded and produced a bulging, blue, spice-scented air-mail envelope, which Carlo swiftly grabbed and placed in the drawer of his desk.

"So, *KnowWhere* is a secret site," Markus echoed impatiently.

"Yes, and a great place to dwell. You should try it."

Markus couldn't believe what he was hearing.

"How do I log on?"

"Easy. You know *Erewhon*® right? Not the Sam Butler novel, of course, the commercial joke. . ."

Markus nodded.

"Well, a year or two after the big launch and media frenzy, a rumor began that someone had hacked the site itself and had created another virtual world, literally at the back of *Erewhon*®, called *KnowWhere*. Well, it checked out."

"I still don't understand why I've never heard about it," Markus mumbled, disoriented.

Carlo dispersed the blue cloud of smoke in front of his face with a quick butterfly hand.

"That's because you don't live here. It's the best kept secret of Sorgbjerg. Only the NoCreds know about it. Man, for once, we have something Creds and Cash don't. . . Culture! No way we're going to share that!"

Dr. Sojo and Carlo laughed in unison.

"Why are you telling me about it, then?" Markus asked.

Dr. Sojo's heavy hand collapsed onto Markus' shoulder, actually hurting him.

"Because we know you and you check out, *amigo*. Not that many astronauts who love literature around anymore. . . Speaking of which, what's your cruise speed right now?"

Markus felt the cellophane bag in his pocket.

"About one for two days. I still don't understand not having felt any of the symptoms yet. I mean, I have, but they're very mild and fade away. On the other hand, it's getting more and more difficult to distinguish hallucinations. Some things I remember I am not sure I actually experienced."

Badia moaned as he put his hand under the fabric of her t-shirt.

Dr. Sojo scratched his head and peered at Markus over his thick glasses.

"Stay off it for a while. See if anything happens. I'm still feeling the crash landing, but then again my consumption is moderate. . ."

"Back to *KnowWhere*. . . How do I log on?"

"Well, you have to log on to *Erewhon*® first. . . Then you go to the virtual Viborg City National Bank building and look for the men's—or the women's—same difference—bathroom. There you click on the door, a black page will appear and ask for a log-on code. Type *Potemkin* and you're in."

"Potemkin?"

"Yes, like the movie. Or rather, like the hackers, you know. . . Some say they escaped from jail and actually created it. . ."

Markus nodded. Carlo handed back the PersoReader. It finally all made sense: the situation was beyond absurd.

✳

The subway stopped, pouring people out, taking new ones in. Staring at the PersoReader between his hands, Markus realized he'd forgotten one thing since he started working for the Man: Power is deaf, blind and mute and it needs people to help it function. But even though Power is a cripple, it denies it and wants people to conform to its fundamentally flawed vision at all costs. Hence, those working for Power eventually became deaf, blind and mute themselves.

seven. commONPLACE FEaTHERS

The apartment welcomed him like a—
No.
Reality, for once.
Synth offered a soda vending machine.

✳

KnowWhere
Nowhere
What a fucking joke.

✳

Paranoia hit Markus the second he logged on to *Erewhon*®.
What if there were hidden cameras in his apartment? What if
Sørensen had organized a 24 hour watch on him?

Synth scanned the surroundings, found nothing—which
made him feel a little better. Synth was reliable radar, for sure (he
hadn't known that before—yet more amazing functionality).

Synth was good.

Synth was his only friend.

Image of a laughing baby.

He steered his avatar among the virtual crowd like a
talented puppeteer.

✳

The bench was empty. Of course the bench was empty. No more
Gloria and Gloria no more. His hands on her breasts, holding
onto them as he came in her in several quick deliciously painful
salvoes. If he had. Synth re-ran the video. He must have. The
phone in his pocket, useless. Later. He was on a mission now,
standing like a pixilated idiot in front of the empty bench.

She said she would buy a computer, first thing.

When?

A NoCred now.

He was on a mission. No time to think.

The virtual Viborg City National Bank stood in front of him,
a few virtual meters away from the virtual bench. He had never
noticed it before. Or had he suppressed it, like a subconscious
symbol of everything he secretly hated but couldn't afford to
acknowledge?

THE SONG OF SYNTH

To forget is to hate.
Karen screaming in the bathroom.
He pressed on, floating in 1204 x 768.

✗

Here he was. The men's room.

The only one not to know about it.

Two, with Sørensen.

The joke didn't make him smile.

He looked around, but the place was empty. *Sinister looking bank, but aren't they all? Gimme my money in a paper bag, quick. Keep the engine running and let's synchronize watches. I would like to have a word with you about your credit, sir. Stool pigeon, you schmuck.*

Black sweat.

He clicked on the door.

A black page, as Dr. Sojo had said.

His fingers hesitatingly descended onto the keys.

Potemkin.

He waited for a few seconds and the screen went black again. Letters appeared, as if typed by an invisible hand.

What is your name?

"Markus."

Who recommended you?

Markus felt his hands become sweaty. Dr. Sojo hadn't mentioned the welcome test.

"Dr. Sojo."

Black screen. More sweat.

Choose your avatar.

It took him almost twenty minutes to decide on his avatar and he hadn't even looked at all the choices. All the major film and comic characters were there, plus a few hundred customized ones. Markus finally chose Dirty Harry because there was something weirdly conservative in the corduroy suit that he really liked.

He clicked on the "save and exit" button and found himself staring at the Viborg City central station. It was an excellent reproduction of the main square, with an incredible array of avatars strolling by—famous actors, literary and comic book characters, monsters and self-designed whatevers. He took a few steps and wondered if Synth was playing some nasty trick on him, but staring around his room, he realized that everything seemed to be normal. Markus focused on the computer screen and took Norbrandt Avenue, to the left of the station.

The reconstruction of the city attained incredible precision and was probably based on genuine army satellite pictures. Of course, you could see the pixels as you neared a wall or an object, but the illusion was still incredible. Then something caught his eye: there were stores, just as in real life, but they weren't the same stores. He knew there should be a *Books and Wonders* bookstore at the corner of Norbrandt and Stangerup, but here it was replaced by the *Yellow Rose Press Bookshop*. Intrigued, he walked up to it and entered.

There were three download terminals. Two were occupied by Captain America and Krazy Kat avatars, he took the vacant one. He clicked on the *Novels* page and a list of titles completely unknown to him scrolled before his eyes. Even more incredible, in a way, all the books were downloadable for almost nothing—you could actually choose how little you wanted to pay.

He walked from the shop stunned, checking out other stores. There were music stores, political bookstores and organic food stores. There were newspapers. There were exchange markets.

A parallel world with a parallel economy, thriving under the surface of the most commercial virtual world on the planet. . . What would Sørensen think about that? Synth materialized a pipe. *No, seriously.* And they didn't know about it.

The lost opportunities of the last ten years suddenly hit him full force, like a train colliding at top speed with a gas truck. *Noise of scraping metal. A brutal shockwave. Explosion. Primary colors. Black smoke.* Where had he been? What had he been doing? Synth opened a catalogue of memories with corresponding background music, but Markus closed it in a rage. Now he knew how it must feel to wake up from a coma. Wonderful dreams but nothing compared with the harsh colors of reality. *What reality? Karen screaming in the bathroom. My name's not Mahdou. Who were you talking to? You fuck. Karen computers hated. You fucking fuck.*

He remembered his old, two-room apartment, up on the 5th floor of Bergmanvej 63, right behind the station. On summer mornings he would open the window and watch the suburban trains roll along the tracks like lazy silkworms. He would smoke a cigarette and think of Karen. Those were happy days. Those were days.

✷

The red brick building of Bergmanvej 63 was here and he clicked on the door expecting nothing, but it opened. The entire structure had been recreated. He climbed the stairs to the fifth floor.

His name.

His real name was on the door.

Thomas Wesenberg

A gust of icy wind filled his hollow chest, bringing a stinging veil of tears. How long since? *Ten years, you moron.* The name tag was a picture of the real one, scribbled with a blue pen and badly taped onto the door. Karen had often asked him why he hadn't done a nicer job. Every time he had shrugged it off. Now he knew: so that it would be unforgettable.

✳

Three loud knocks on the door. Ole's round face and sweet blue eyes, Mona Lisa, feminine half-smile and huge shoulders bending in through the door, hands never empty—a bottle of wine, whisky, whatever, joyously lifted up as a salute. Then Nick's discreet tapping. The small silhouette shuffling in and the dark page-boy hair. Blue eyes also, staring right through him. Karen in the kitchen preparing food, a salad usually in the summer, lasagna in the winter. Rituals of conspiracy. Never say too much in front of Karen—no need to drag innocents into this. Much good, it had done... Of course, she wasn't stupid—she saw the computers and when she finally went to bed, after kissing him gently on the lips, she could probably still hear their muted conversations as she fell asleep. It had been a good thing she had hated computers so much. Prevented her from understanding what was *really* going on—and made it easier for him to lie. He would join her in bed hours later, pressing his body against hers, as if she was an indestructible shield.

✳

He clicked on the tag and a window appeared.
Leave a message.
Not really knowing why, he typed a few words.
"Honey, I'm home."
And it didn't even make him smile.

✳

Gloria. Badia. A NoCred now. Did she know about *KnowWhere*? Would be ironic, to say the least. A computer, she would buy first thing she had said. Her nipples, a dark brown. Why was he in this taxi, zooming back to her place? The smell of leather, probably. A smile? He wanted to know. To make sure. Had he or hadn't he? Her dark body rubbing against his, her soft stomach and her deep navel accepting him as a new earth and sky.

✳

"Oh, it's you."
"Yes."
The flatness of real language. He missed *Erewhon*® and the keyboard conversations. Did she realize?
"Come in."

The voice was weary. *Had they?* He stayed where he was, hesitating.

"I tried to call you," he explained, "but I think I wrote down the number wrong."

"Well, it was pretty late when you left. And we were pretty drunk. . ."

She laughed and it echoed pleasantly in his ears.

"I have a question. . ." he began, feeling his words flying ahead of him like stray bullets.

"Why don't you ask me inside? There are more beers in the fridge."

Markus nodded, his throat dry, and stepped once again into the crammed two-room apartment, with the red sofa and small TV.

He sat down and she joined him with two cans of chilled beer.

"Okay," she said, opening her beer. "What do you want to know?"

She was sitting very close to him, her knee touching his. *Blue sparks. The hum of electricity. Maybe they had, after all. Quick, another question.*

"Have you ever heard of a virtual world called KnowWhere?"

She shook her head.

"No. Why?"

That made three of them. Markus felt relieved.

"Someone mentioned it to me, but I've never heard of it either. It's supposedly a secret site, where you can get a lot of illegal stuff. . ."

She balanced her beer on her lap, her deep brown eyes dancing over his face.

"You mean like pedophile images?"

"No, like music, books, cultural things. . ."

She smiled, obviously relieved.

"Could be nice. Hate the shit we hear on the radio. Well, I'd have to buy a computer first. You know they take everything from you when you become a NoCred and replace it with government issue appliances? It's on credit of course— deducted from your pay check. If you save money you can get more things. Like a computer."

Markus remained silent, embarrassed by the confession.

"They just found me a job at the public library. In the cafeteria. If all goes well I should be able to get a new computer in four years and an internet connection in five. . . Unless, of course, I get to know someone who knows someone. . . No wonder the black market is so big around here. . . Even bigger than in Samarqand, if you can imagine. . ."

Markus nodded. He would give her the names of Dr. Sojo and Carlo. They knew people. Of course, Dr. Sojo could also turn her into a junkie. . .

"How did you become a NoCred, by the way? I don't know if I asked you this question before—like you said, I was so drunk I don't even know how I got home. . ."

Nice lie. You took a cab. You can't remember if you fucked her, that's different.

"I had an accident and had the wrong sort of insurance. Didn't cover the costs."

Markus remembered a long period without Gloria. A month, maybe more. Everything had a rational explanation. She had said she had travelled. Why doubt?

Her perfume floated around him like an aura. He put down his beer and turned towards her. Her face was so close he couldn't see it any more.

✳

Badia's body was fantastic. He couldn't believe he was against her, naked, in her bed. Her breasts were soft under his hands, only the nipples hard and willing. Her back, a long curve. The angle of her hips, perfect against his. They weren't machines, programs, citizens. They were naked and making love. This time for real.

For real?

Yes.

Synth ran in a parallel world. False memories were becoming real. Just as he had wrongly remembered, she hadn't cared about the anklet, just remarked on it before letting him lie down next to her. *Wrongly remembered?* No, foreseen. Was Synth a psychic drug or was he just becoming crazy? Image of his face exploding in a thousand puzzle pieces, like in a bad 70s psychedelic flick. Exactly. He heard cithara and tambourines. Black sweat. Was he coming down, finally, between Badia's arms? Quicksilver thoughts. A flash of panic. Dr. Sojo, so many questions. Answers, anyone?

✳

"Tell me about Samarqand," he said, accepting her cigarette.

She offered him a light, then settled down next to him exhaling a blue cloud.

"Why? You planning your holidays?"

THE SONG OF SYNTH

They laughed. Samarqand was the last place one chose for a holiday. It was the city of the Enemy, although no war had officially been declared. It was mysterious, incomprehensible, formidable. Exotic, religious and hateful, yet it had the nerve to call itself *democratic*. There were indeed elections every four years. Exactly like in Viborg City, Babylon, Petersburg and all other megalopoli of the civilized world—but they knew what elections in Samarqand really meant: *corruption and lies.*

Yet it also held the reputation of being one of the most beautiful cities in the world, along with Ur and Xanadu. The Blue Walls were famous, as well as Temudjin's yellow marble palace. There were old documentaries, travelogues and propaganda films. But since the war, ten years ago, and Samarqand's support to South-East China, all contacts except mandatory diplomatic ones had been severed.

Things had gradually improved over the years, as the king granted more democratic rights, such as press and religious freedom.

Immigrants had started to reappear in all major cities—but they were different. In the past there had also been immigrants—political refugees who openly criticized the tyrannical regimes in their homelands and organized governments in exile ready to seize power once hypothetical revolutions had taken place. The new immigrants (who started arriving four years ago) were economic ones—sometimes with university degrees (useless in Viborg City, of course), but often with nothing but hope and courage. They caused a new problem, not because of their number—the borders and airports were tightly controlled—but because of their political stance—or rather their non-political

103

stance—they didn't criticize Samarqand any more, merely talked about its poverty and the difficulties of daily life.

For the governments of the Western Coalition, Babylon, Petersburg, Viborg City and all the other major European megalopoli, Samarqand was still an enemy city to which it was all but forbidden to travel—but the immigrants integrated well and spoke not of horrors and oppressions, but of economic problems caused by the Western Coalition's blockade.

Recently these immigrants had been the target of many political attacks, both from the Conservatives and the Progressists, being accused of everything that was going wrong in the Western Coalition, from unemployment and social instability to being the fifth column preparing to overthrow democracy. . .

"Actually," Markus said, "I'd love to visit it, some day."

Which was true. He had often dreamt of Samarqand while in prison—to him it was like the unattainable symbol of freedom. The exotic other. A place in which to become really invisible.

"It's beautiful," Badia agreed. "The Blue Walls, especially. And the old city. My family lives in the suburbs. They can see Temudjin's mausoleum from the window of their apartment."

"Why did you come to Viborg City? I mean, it's cold, gray and not that exciting. . ."

Badia sat up in bed, reaching for an ashtray.

"Well, I had finished university, with a degree in economics in a ruined country. . . What else could I do? Get married to a cousin and do the bookkeeping at his grocery?"

She laughed dryly. Markus let a finger run down from her shoulder to the small of her back. He loved her smell. Samarqand.

"And now? I mean. . ."

She scratched her thick hair with her beautiful hand and stared back at him, her brown eyes catching his in a friendly embrace.

"It's still better to be a NoCred here than unemployed in my city. Especially if you're a woman."

Markus took a long drag on his cigarette, and watched her slowly disappear behind the smokescreen.

✷

This time it had been real, no question about it. Dawn was rising over the gray roofs of the Strindberg Residence. He noticed a beautiful white feather gently shivering on the first step of his stairs. He picked it up and looked at it with all his tired attention. *Real.*

✷

The office. Him within. Synth within him within. Where was Synth? It felt like it had disappeared for the last hour or so. But what about the withdrawal symptoms? What about the black sweat and the feeling of guilt? He sat on his chair in front of the computer and thought of Samarqand.

The Blue Walls surrounded him in all their ancient glory, slightly hazy because of the sun. He stared at them, breathless, and turned Synth off. It was still there, somewhere.

Within his office.

✳

Black sweat was back. The CashCard was in the safe and the PersoReader on the desk next to the computer. Sørensen wouldn't accept failure but could Markus tell him about *KnowWhere*? Could he give up something he would have loved to have imagined himself, during the days of the Potemkin Crew?

Markus suddenly felt extremely tired.

Of course, he had only slept a couple of hours next to Badia last night—a quick shower in her NoCred bathroom and into the subway—no change of clothes—yesterday's stale sweat clinging to him like a second shadow—but he knew the tiredness, the *profound* tiredness came from somewhere else. Conscience. Choices. Morality.

Synth sketched out Chartres Cathedral.

He stood up and took the credit card from the safe, waving at the tiny eye of the surveillance camera. He inserted it in the peripheral slot and stared at the data again. Anonymous. No identification, but billions accredited. A skeleton key for— what, whom? What was the link with *KnowWhere*? Why was Christensen dead? Who was Jean Gray?

Something suddenly clicked.

KnowWhere. Jean Gray. X-Men. Avatars.

Christensen had told them Jean Gray had given him the card. If he found Jean Gray in *KnowWhere*'s database, then he would find out her identity. Of course. As simple as that.

As if.

106

He laughed out loud.

Yeah, as if.

✳

As soon as he stepped into his apartment, he noticed the "you have mail" notice flashing on his computer screen. *Sørensen, no doubt.* He had left work early today, telling the secretary he wasn't feeling well—which was perfectly true. He was feeling exhausted, depressed and paranoid. And the notice on the flat screen didn't help.

He walked directly to his computer, without even taking his wet jacket off. Still standing, he clicked on his email box and frowned in surprise. The message was from Cyber Magic® Inc. Could it be because of his *KnowWhere* escapade? Had he been traced?

He read the message, heart beating heavily.

It was an invitation to meet with Cyber Magic®'s founder and C.E.O., Kristin Hansen, tomorrow morning at 10:00. He wasn't supposed to reply to this message if he accepted the appointment. He lifted a hand then let it drop again.

A job offer, maybe?

eight. aniMALS

Dr. Sojo was waiting for him outside the AK Bar, his legendary green Parka tightly wrapped around his formidable body. The bar's sharp lights thinned his silhouette somewhat, casting a blurred and elongated shadow on the sidewalk. The good doctor offered him a thin joint by way of greeting. The tip glowed dimly in the drizzle. A tiny red light among artificial suns.

*

No friends. In the last ten years, Markus had lived in a silvery bubble all by himself. And then, suddenly—Dr. Sojo's phone call tonight inviting him to a free concert. Something like the good old days. Ole and Nick, drinking buddies, music lovers, fellow students—and partners in crime. Ghosts over ghosts, feelings layered on other feelings. Karen screaming in the bathroom. A scream that erased everything.

✳

At the bar, Dr. Sojo ordered two imported beers.

"Who is playing?" Markus asked, toasting in a crystalline clash of beer bottle necks.

"Friends of mine. They call themselves 'A.' You can download their album for free on *KnowWhere*."

"Of course."

"Of course."

The music started almost immediately, a two-man band with electronics and guitars. The sound was both familiar and bizarre—Synth-induced no doubt. The audience cheered.

"Are they customers too?" Markus shouted in Dr. Sojo's ear.

"Yes, of course."

"Of course."

Pressed against Dr. Sojo's shoulder, Markus thought of friendship again. What it meant to share, to be with. Sentimental things, bullshit no doubt. Still—he hadn't shared a gig like this for so long.

With the Potemkin Crew, he had been obliged to sever all close ties—parents and family included. The only friends, Ole and Nick. So close. Cellmates almost, like a prediction. And Karen—he stopped Synth just in time. But *normal* contacts were gone, erased from his daily life USB key. After the trial and jail time—even worse. His job and anklet had created a super force-field around him. Now that he had slept with Badia, he realized the force-field had more likely been a mental illusion than anything else—still, reality was reality. No friends.

Apart from Synth.

Something warm and golden rolled inside his head.

The first number was finished. Silver raindrops fading in sunlight. Definitely Synth-music. Maybe Dr. Sojo was right after all—a revolution.

✱

The gig was over and they were sitting at a table now, Dr. Sojo clutching his beer between large hairy fingers. Markus' hands were sore from clapping. A great band. He was glad Dr. Sojo had called him. He would download their album first chance he got. A good reason to visit *KnowWhere* again.

"Still riding, if you don't mind me asking?"

Markus nodded.

"Yeah, amazing."

"No bad vibes?"

Markus shrugged.

"Once in a while, but nothing like before. More like angst attacks, you know the deal. Black sweat."

Dr. Sojo sneered.

"Black sweat. That's a good one. Cool name for a band. Will suggest that to my 'A' friends. Fucking stupid name for such great music. You been to *KnowWhere* by the way?"

"Yes. Quite something."

"Isn't it? Great place to run a business. And you can find so many things. And interesting people. I even met people from Samarqand there."

"Wow!"

Markus took a long gulp of his lukewarm pilsner. His mind was racing. Who was he now? Markus Olsen? Thomas Olsen? Synth flashed excerpts from *Dr Jekyll and Mr. Hyde*. Jekyll prevailed. If Olsen was indeed Jekyll. . .

"By the way, speaking of *KnowWhere*, do you know anybody there using a Jean Gray avatar?"

"Why? You fallen in love?"

"Maybe. . ."

Dr. Sojo frowned and scratched his head. Markus wondered for a second what would happen if Dr. Sojo noticed his anklet. *The end of a friendship, you fuck.* Well, he could lie like he had lied to Badia. He had become an expert in lies. The trickster. Had even tricked himself.

"No. There are so many people out there. Doesn't ring a bell. What's yours, by the way?—Maybe we'll meet some day."

"Dirty Harry."

"Always thought there was a fascist hiding in you. . . Why Dirty Harry?"

"Because of the corduroy suit and the free jazz film score. . . What's yours?"

"Alice in Wonderland."

"Of course."

"Of course."

They toasted.
"Old friends."
You fuck.

✷

The Cyber Magic® headquarters lay on Dronning Margrethesvej, the super wealthy area of Viborg City, three subway stops away from the Viborg Security building and fifteen from his flat in the Strindberg Residence. It was an old nineteenth century luxury hotel turned into a business office centre. Markus had called in sick again—Sørensen would have to wait for now.

Crossing the street from the subway station, he noticed a newsstand. The headlines were all about the elections taking place tomorrow. He had completely forgotten about them. The Prime Minister who had agreed to send the nation head first into the South Eastern Chinese War disaster was a Social-Liberal. Olsen, the National-Liberal, had been elected while Markus sat in prison. Markus began to whistle *A las Barricadas*. It was the first time the tune had crossed his lips in ten years. It felt naive and it felt good. Real good. Real naive, too.

At reception he gave his name to a uniformed, balding receptionist and was directed to the elevators. Cyber Magic® occupied the top two floors. Miss or Mrs. Hansen's office was on the top floor.

He entered a room where the blue leather furniture smelled new and oily and was welcomed by a secretary—a blonde woman uselessly wearing thick designer glasses to make her look less plain.

He gave his name to the young woman, who checked her computer screen.

"Yes, Mr. Olsen. You can sit down. Miss Hansen will see you soon."

Markus sat and skimmed through the fashion magazines arranged on the glass table. A job? Questions about *KnowWhere*? Had they traced him? Were they a front for the secret service?

Synth built up his old prison cell.

No, impossible.

Sørensen would have told him, wouldn't he? *Pipe fart. You fucking fuck. Elections tomorrow. To vote is your duty. Nothing is free, everything has a price. To download is to steal. Make sure your copy is officially certified. To download is anarchy. Out of control. To vote is your duty. Remember to push the right button on the machine. I promise. A new era. Freedom and justice. Democracy is choice. Regular or black? Sugar? Can Sørensen see anything without his glasses?*

"Mr. Olsen?"

The secretary's voice snapped him out of his paranoid reverie. A Synth crash-landing. Finally. He felt relieved. Wasn't completely infected yet. Still some good old blood running in his veins. A few synapses left.

"Miss Hansen is ready to see you."

She opened a door and showed him in. The office was gigantic, with an impressive 1930s ebony desk and assorted chairs.

A framed original 1917 Russian revolution poster hung on the wall above a functional leather armchair—Miss Hansen wasn't in yet.

He stared at the poster, nonplussed. It showed a Budyenni Cossack riding his horse, saber drawn, on a stylized background

113

of city and countryside. It was a strange image to have in the office of one of the largest international internet companies. Maybe it was ironic. Or maybe Miss Hansen was an ignorant who just happened to like the image. *A las Barricadas* crossed his lips again and Synth produced the Spanish Civil war, with running anarchist militiamen and a rain of fascist bullets.

"So it's really you. . ."

He recognized the voice before his consciousness could actually register it. He turned around and his neurons short-circuited behind his eyes.

Karen.

Karen screaming in the bathroom.

"Of course, you've changed, but I would recognize you anywhere," she said, bemused. "The way you hunch a little to the left and your sagging ass. . ."

Karen. Ten years older, short-haired and dressed as a National-Liberal deputy in her deep gray ensemble. . . But the same dark eyes and half-smile. . . Markus felt so dizzy he had to sit.

"Don't sit, we're going out for coffee."

He stood back up like a zombie.

If she had told him to jump through the window, he would have done so without a split second of hesitation.

Synth gave him beautiful butterfly wings.

This time, he accepted them.

✱

To Markus' surprise, Karen didn't take him to a fancy café, but to a normal one, where people talked loudly and waiters stank of sweat and French fries.

She ordered an espresso and he did the same. Bitter black energy was exactly what he needed right now. Was Synth playing with him? Was this real? He felt like pinching her to make sure, but he remembered that Synth-induced hallucinations played with *all* the senses, touch included.

"Are you real?"

The words departed from his lips like an accidental shot. More control or he was going to hurt somebody. Himself, to be sure.

Karen laughed her old Karen laugh, bringing invisible tears to his eyes.

"Of course I'm real! But I know what you mean. . . It's the same for me, seeing you here. . . When did you get out of jail?"

Never.

Or had he?

"Some time ago. You didn't know?"

As if. Who knew? His release hadn't been advertised. It was a *secret d'état*, well protected by all sorts of disinformation methods, such as pseudo-mail interviews with journalists and other bright tricks. He had actually given a *telephone* interview from his *prison parlor* to some foreign paper three weeks ago.

Karen shook her head.

"And you?" he asked. "What happened?"

She looked around, as if she was afraid of being overheard.

"I have so many things to tell you. So many. . . But you've got to tell me how you got out of prison. . . Did you escape? Where were you hiding?"

It was Markus' turn to look around for eavesdroppers.

"I don't know if I can tell you. . . I mean. . . Why did you send me an email?"

"Because of your message on the door."

"How did you trace me?"

Karen smiled.

"Everybody leaves a trace. You know that."

Markus nodded. Only the truth hurt. Everybody did leave a trace. An IP number, a lipstick smudge or a fingerprint. No one was safe. No one. He knew that.

"I wanted to know who had written on that door," she resumed. "If it was really you. . . I had to check. . ."

She seemed uneasy, embarrassed almost. Her slightly blushing cheeks made her even more beautiful. Too beautiful, maybe. *Yes, maybe. You fucking fuck.*

Markus took a deep breath. He was standing at the edge of a cliff, with a powerful wind slapping his face. Below the sea was crashing ashore and the rocks looked like small, shiny black stones. Where were the wings Synth had given him?

"Are you Jean Gray?"

Her eyes met his and locked.

"Who are you working for?"

Markus moved uneasily on his chair.

"It's a long story."

"I think I know it. Or I can imagine it."

They stared at each other, or rather through each other. Faces overlapping, locations unraveling, memories, bits and pieces, flesh, raw meat, a few hairs, life, the past, dust, rain, the possibility of seasons. . .

"Are you wearing a wire?" she asked, calmly.

Markus smiled painfully.

"Hell, no! Are you?"

"No. But do you want to check?"

Her eyes held his questioning gaze. Markus felt the world tilt at an impossible angle. His head hit the surface of the water. Salt invaded his lips.

"Yes," he said. "Sure. I want to check."

*

The hotel room welcomed them as a hotel always did, anonymous and slightly smelling of dust, although it was clean and functional: a bed, a side table, a chair and, of course, a TV on the wall at the end of the bed. Karen pulled the curtains, turning the gray morning light a dull yellowish shade.

She moved softly towards Markus, taking his hands in hers. She smelled of rain and gas fumes. The smell of winter when winter was familiar. Their mouths met without hesitation. His hands lifted her shirt and stroked her burning back.

"See?" she whispered. "No wire."

*

Markus hesitated when she opened his jeans. Karen felt his hesitation and drew back a few inches, her hands still on his belt.

"Is there a problem? A wife? A girlfriend?"

Markus shook his head.

"This."

He bent over and lifted the right leg of his jeans. The anklet.

"Now you know who I am working for."

Karen smiled and kissed him.

"That's what I figured. Like your new job?"

Markus shook his head.

"I hate it."

"That's what I figured too."

Markus' pants dropped to his ankles. The anklet disappeared for a moment.

✳

It was still raining outside. Synth could have turned the sinister room into a palace in Marrakech, but Karen was in his arms and that was stronger than any hallucination. Time was going forward again. *The acceleration of particles. Karen. Or Kristin. Gloria. Or Badia. Marcus. Or Thomas. Identities. Lies. Avatars. Mirror moves.* Karen lifted her head and drew him closer. Another kiss. Harder this time. He had remembered her in t-shirt and jeans. She had changed so much. How had she remembered him?

Parenthesis:

He had remembered her in t-shirt and jeans. Was it true? Or was it a memory he had chosen to keep, an icon of some sorts? What about the many fights, the bitterness, the subtle remarks about "not sharing the daily chores enough" and the "reactionary machismo of his best buddies?"

Close parenthesis.

How had she remembered him?

Second parenthesis:

Evening meals watching TV. A shower, the sound of water on her body and the faint smell of her body lotion. The suggestion of her cleft and dark pubic hair as she read a newspaper in her t-shirt and underwear on the sofa, one leg up against the coffee-table. A conversation, laughter. Rain ceasing to be an existential problem. Cheek against cheek, looking forward like in a revolutionary poster.

Close second parenthesis, perhaps overlapping the first.

"Do you want to work for me?" she asked, stroking the top of his thigh with a soft hand.

"What?"

True?

Untrue?

"Do you want to work for me?"

True.

Does truth have an echo?

Markus heard the rain on the window. A much clearer sound than earlier. Echo of an echo.

"What do you mean?"

Exactly.

Karen sat up in bed. He admired her beautiful back. She hadn't changed that much. Her body, he meant. She could still wear jeans and a t-shirt.

"I mean just that. Do you want to work for me?"

"For Cyber Magic®? I can't."

She turned her head around and smiled. It was a new smile, one he had never seen before. Hard, direct, knowing. A Goddess. Athena. A bronze shield.

"No, for *KnowWhere*."

Markus smiled and pointed at his ankle.

"You know I can't. I can't run away."

She nodded and grabbed his cigarettes from the side table.

"Still smoking these?" she said.

Amused. In control.

Synth suggested a computer from the fifties, with blinking lights.

She lit a cigarette and handed him the pack. He fished one out, lit it from hers. Their smoke clouds mingled.

"They want you to believe you can't."

Markus exhaled.

"It's a GPS tracker device. It's real."

"You can take it off. Do it. For five minutes. See what happens."

"I can't take it off! It's locked!"

Karen bent over his leg and reached for the black device. She searched for something with her fingers and pushed. There was a click and the anklet fell off.

"See? You're free."

Markus' mouth dropped open. The world spun at incredible speed. Gravitation was pulling him down, although he was slowly floating upwards. Impossible. Free. Synth creaked like a rusty wheel. A searchlight behind his eyes.

Sørensen: What do you mean: 'you lost him'?

He reached for the anklet in a panic. He looked at the mechanism. Shut the bracelet around thin air. *Click!* Pressed on the button. Opened it again. *Click!* Same sound, same wavelength.

"Every slave misses his collar," Karen said. "I know. I've been there too."

Suddenly Markus felt even more naked than he really was. He was free and freedom was a nightmare. Karen was back and that was a nightmare too. *What do you mean you?*

"Have you ever wondered how Sørensen tracked you down?" she asked, scratching her head with the back of her thumb.

"Every day," Markus answered, like an automaton. "Every single day. Still wonder who their hacker was. . ."

Karen smiled sadly.

"There was no hacker, Thomas. There was only me."

Thomas. His old name. His old name.

"Sørensen had me too. Thirty years if I didn't cooperate. I ran a peer-to-peer network, about a year before they sent me in your direction. The best one. Quicksilver Clouds. Remember?"

Markus nodded. Who hadn't used it? The site was shut down and those behind it were given long prison sentences. Well, so the media had said. A great corporate victory. He'd marched in the streets during the Pirate Riots following the trial.

"Sørensen was curious about you. He'd heard things. Rumors. Activists, possibly second generation hackers. You know how it works. University is a small place. He wanted to check. So he sent me. For you. And we met."

The puzzle was in place. Markus felt like the Greek general hopefully asking about his future before a battle, and hearing he will die. Who needed the truth? *You fuck. You fucking fuck.*

"I turned you in, Thomas. And Ole and Nick too. That's why I never came to visit you in prison. My job was done and I had signed a contact in which it was clearly specified that I must never, ever contact you again."

Karen screaming in the bathroom. Sørensen smoking his pipe. We want names. This is not a test. I repeat, this is not a test.

"So we're both fucked now," Markus said, taking a long drag on what remained of his cigarette.

"No," Karen said, curling up against him, the smell of her raw nakedness jumping once again to his tobacco-filled nostrils. "*They're* fucked."

She turned on the TV. A documentary about lions. They were eating a dead antelope. Yellow grass, red meat, white eyeballs. How perfect.

Markus' thoughts crashed into each other in blurred chaos. Stalingrad. Synth evoked ruins. Explosions. Running shadows. A sense of panic and a desire for victory.

"Who was Christensen?"

Karen killed her cigarette.

"They set you on him?"

Markus shook his head.

"No, I tracked him and then they set me on him."

"The moron," she said.

"What happened? Who was he?"

Karen shrugged her beautiful shoulders. Markus noticed she had put on some weight and that her breasts were sagging a little. *Enjoy reality. My treat, for free.*

"He worked for me. For us. *KnowWhere*. It's an organization, you know. Not just a portal. Anyway, Bjørn was in logistics. I didn't want to give him the card and. . ."

She stopped, aware of having said too much. Markus smiled reassuringly.

"Don't worry. I know about that."

Karen nodded.

"Okay. . . Well, I didn't trust him one hundred percent. I thought he was too young and could do stupid things with it. But he insisted. He wanted to see if it worked and offered himself in sacrifice. The others supported him—he was a popular figure in our movement. A rising star. So I finally gave in. And the idiot got caught. . . How did you find him by the way?"

"Viborg City National Bank security systems. He probably wanted to check if the card had been traced. They found some recent receipts at his apartment."

Karen looked for another cigarette. Her pager chimed on the floor. She didn't even flinch.

"Yes, I guess you're right. The dumb fuck. Always told him to stick to what he knew and not try to mess with computers. . . But he was young and wanted to prove he could, I guess. . . Male virility bullshit. . ."

Markus saw something flicker in her eyes and heard the fake irony in her tone.

"Your lover?"

She shrugged.

"Only recently. I was getting tired of being the Corporate Virgin."

"You created Cyber Magic®?"

No surprise. Beyond surprise now. Little Karen asking him stupid questions about his computer stuff. If he had only known. She could have been a great asset to the Potemkin Crew.

"Yes. A cunning plan."

A vicious smile.

"After your arrest, my contract was fulfilled. Pocketed the reward and began thinking. I had lived with you for almost two years. You got me thinking. You opened my eyes— or rather, confirmed what I was seeing. Love can do that, sometimes."

The hotel room expanded, as if it had taken a deep breath.

"Love?" Markus asked, his heart suddenly made of glass.

Oh, fragile little me. Did you fuck her?

"Love. I created *Erewhon*® and *KnowWhere* back to back, to avenge you. And redeem myself. Remorse, they call it."

Markus focused on a crack in the ceiling. It was a very thin crack, but a crack nonetheless. Imperceptible almost, but running along the full width of the ceiling.

"Sørensen gave me Christensen's PersoReader along with the card. Who wrote *The Potemkin Overture*?"

"Ole. He's in Samarqand now. Or so the rumor goes. Escaped four years ago. Don't you watch the news?"

Information overdose. All systems are down. No, he hadn't watched or read the news in the last ten years. Had tried not to at least. Apparently, with some success.

"And Nick?"

She lit the cigarette she was dancing in front of her face like a white moth.

"Nick's dead. He was diabetic. He went into a coma, shortly after the trial. You didn't know that either?"

"No, I didn't."

Silence. *Reality equals death.*

A prick in the silvery bubble.

Pop! goes the weasel.

Shuffle the cards one more time. This time, what? A pair? A full house? Hoping for a flush?

"The CashCard," she said after a long pause filled with silently screaming ghosts. "Do you know where it is?"

Sørensen behind his desk, pipe stuck in the corner of his mouth. The prison cell, walls painted a nightmarish gray. A cloud of pipe smoke. Poker, anyone?

"Yes."

"Can it be recovered?"

Markus shook his head.

"It's in a safe, watched by a video-camera."

"Can it be destroyed?"

Can I be destroyed? Of course. Anybody can. A pleasure to meet you. Karen screaming in the bathroom. The door explodes. I am destroyed. I am destroyed. I am a door.

"Karen, did you have Christensen killed?"

There was surprise in her eyes.

"Karen. . . I love it when you say this name. . ."

Markus welcomed her kiss. *You do not reject water. You do not reject air. You do not reject food. You do not reject a gift.*

"Answer me."

He wanted her again. She felt his erection and extended a hand.

"Answer me."

"He had become a liability. We voted. I voted against. I was the only one. I remember the stares. Where is the card?"

"In my office."

The ground is approaching at incredible speed.

"Can you get it back?"

I can see trees. I can see houses. I can see people.

Markus shook his head.

"If I get it back, then Sørensen will know. And I will be fucked."

"You are fucked."

"I will be even more fucked."

"Let's do it then."

125

Her mouth enfolded his penis in its moist, warm blanket. *I can see nothing.*

∗

"*That credit card, what is it for? I mean, what is its purpose?*"

"*Subversion, what else?*"

"*How does it work? I couldn't trace it to anything.*"

"*Ha, ha… Have you heard about Synth?*"

Shockwave. Back in the subway. The time, what time is it? Half past twelve. Black sweat. Karen's body. A true memory. Is it? Yes.

"Yes."

"*It's a military drug. Based on the brain's algorithms. It follows them, for maximum effect. Like a virus. It adapts. The purpose was to help each soldier maximize his inherent capabilities. Only problem: it was uncontrollable. Soldiers went insane, some disappeared completely, others pretended they were becoming psychic and could hear other people's thoughts… A mess…*"

"*How do you know that?*"

"*My father invented Synth, He also designed the card. It's based on the same principle. It adapts. It changes all the time. He found a way to break binary logic. It goes 0-2 or 0-4 or 0-0. Invisible. Opens all doors. My father was also a composer. He wrote ultra and infra-sound symphonies. He had just died when I met you and my mother never threw away his computer. I loved my father. I really did.*"

The Shakespearian moment. What is truth? Words, I say. Words are said. Karen hating computers. Karen screaming in the bathroom. Karen talking, naked in my arms. Markus'? Thomas's? Arms? *I am sorry, is that your hat?* Rumble of the train.

The tracks elongate and thin under the weight of the metal carriage. Home is a few stops away. Or the illusion of home.

Shuffle the cards once again. Why did he always get a bad hand? What was he playing, anyway? Poker? Bridge? Crazy eights?

Her father.

What now?

Synth.

Her father.

Stuck in the labyrinth with a defective map. The Minotaur, a possibility at every corner.

His hand lowered to his ankle. The anklet was still in place. His fingers felt the switch. Karen had shown him how. The possibility of invisibility. Freedom?

Call or raise?

The train stopped and the doors slid open.

Like an animal at the zoo, he contemplated the odds of the opened doors, counting time backwards.

nine. WAiTiNG ON THE LINE

Carlo was sorting books from a large cardboard box as Markus walked in. The comfort of pages. The warmth of paper.

"You're early," the bookseller said, in his deadpan tone. "I just opened."

The clock over the counter—a circular, black and white, vintage hospital clock—indicated one thirty in the afternoon. Markus had never known Carlo's opening hours, as he usually came late in the evening. *Ignorance is bliss. I only know that I know nothing.*

"I was passing by . . . Didn't go to work today. . . I need a thick book."

Carlo frowned, rubbing his chin.

"Can you be a little more specific?"

"A book that can be read in many different ways. Exotic would be a plus."

Carlo scratched his head.

"I can see a light."

"A book with a lot of doors and no walls."

"Then I have exactly what you need."

Carlo dropped the book he was holding back into the box and took a couple of steps sideways, scrutinizing the multicolored shelves. A few seconds later he found a thick sim-leather bound volume.

"Lawrence Durrell, *The Alexandria Quartet*. Ugly edition, but complete. Fairly rare nowadays."

Markus took the book. It was heavy.

"What's it about?"

"Everything. Tragic love. Murder. Betrayal. A city. Time. Perspective. Women. Hare lip."

Markus opened the first page and read a few lines. The words were vibrating like an enchanting melody. *Subsonic. My father. Karen screaming in the bathroom.* Justine. *Lovely name.*

"I'll take it."

"Want some mint-tea?"

"Please. Have you seen Dr. Sojo?"

Carlo shook his head as he poured boiling water into two small glasses on his desk, being careful not to spill.

"Not today. He might be at home. He might not be. His life is like a book randomly opened every day."

"Aren't you the true philosopher?"

Carlo smiled, a glimpse of white teeth above his dark chin.

"Sugar?"

✳

Dr. Sojo was indeed at home. He didn't have his parka on, for once, and was wearing only pants and a sleeveless white t-shirt. His arms were covered with crude, prison tattoos.

"Can I come in? I've got some information for you."

"Are you having a bad trip?" the Doctor asked, his dark eyes piercing through the round glasses.

Markus shook his head.

"Info, you said? You're making me very curious."

Dr. Sojo let Markus into his den. The shutters were drawn and a heavy smell of weed pervaded the room. Moroccan music hummed softly in the background and Markus wondered if the doctor would offer him some mint-tea too.

They sat opposite each other, on the smelly leather stools. Dr. Sojo grunted as he collapsed onto his.

"I'm getting too old for this shit. So? The info?"

Markus told him as best he could what Karen had told him about Synth, taking care not to mention her name.

"The scientific part escapes me, but pragmatic experimentation would seem to confirm the facts. . . Does it mean this is a dangerous drug?"

Markus shrugged.

"I don't know."

"Better that way don't you think? You want a mint-tea?"

✷

The secretary shot him a surprised look.

"I thought you were ill."

"I've still got a slight fever, but there's something I absolutely have to check. Work, you know."

She nodded, as if she understood *exactly* what he meant. *Coming to work with the flu. First time in ten years. Sørensen would love that. Maybe give him a raise. Freedom? Of course, freedom.*

✳

He opened the safe and took the card out, waving as usual.

✳

Time had changed. Seconds had turned into minutes and minutes into hours. Slow motion without the blur. *A film?*

✳

In the subway, he read once more the SMS he had just received.

If you accept my proposition, meet me you know where. Jean Gray.

X-Men. Karen had explained her father had collected comics since his childhood and that the X-Men seemed perfect as a nickname for their organization, which actually had another name. A secret name. Wow. *Welcome to the Labyrinth, Thomas—er, Markus. Keep your eyes and mouth shut tight. Sleep tight. Yeah right.* Members of the O. were the only ones allowed to have X-Men avatars on *KnowWhere*. Made it easier for identification. Markus had never really read comics. *A fault?*

He snapped the cell phone shut, took the SIM-card out and slid it in his pocket. Later, he crushed it with his heel and dropped it through a sewer grate. Karen had finally stopped screaming in the bathroom.

✱

His apartment welcomed him just like it always did.

Markus looked around, holding back Synth which was jumping around him like a happy young dog. *Later. Go fetch.* He opened a cupboard and took out his old sports bag. He hadn't used it in years. Ten years, to be exact. Since he had moved here from his cell. He zipped it open.

✱

Badia found him waiting for her on the stairs. She bent over to kiss him.

"You're going somewhere?" she asked, noticing the bag.

He nodded.

"Time to take that vacation, I think."

Laughing, she took out her keys and unlocked the door.

✱

She opened the window of the bedroom, even though the November night was cold outside.

"I like to hear the traffic," she explained. "It's like the ocean. What's more, people here say it's healthy to sleep in a cold room. Makes you stronger."

Markus was lying in her bed, smoking one of her cigarettes. She joined him and he felt her warm skin brush against his side. The smell of sex floated in the darkness like a spicy breeze.

Badia kissed his neck below the ear.

A warm tongue.

She hadn't remarked on the absence of the anklet and he hadn't told her he had thrown it into the garbage can at the bottom of her stairs.

"You sure you want to go to Samarqand?" she asked. "It's not a great tourist destination."

He sucked on the filter then blew out the smoke in one long cloud.

"I told you I wanted to visit there. An old dream."

"It's a strange place. You might like it actually. You're strange enough to like it."

Markus smiled in the dark and turned to kiss her, but she sat up.

"Let me give you my uncle's address. At least, you'll have someone to show you around. Someone unofficial, I mean."

"You don't have to. . ." he said as she got out of bed.

She wrapped herself in her bathrobe and disappeared into the living-room, turning on the light.

"Here," she said, handing him a piece of paper. "Now, let's make love again. In my country, it is said to ward off evil spirits."

✳

Dawn lifted its rainy curtain over the Herman Bang projects, making the red brick look gray. Standing at the bottom of the stairs of Badia's building, Markus watched the garbage truck drive away, its sweet-sour stench floating around his nostrils. The anklet would probably be crushed in a couple of minutes.

What do you mean: "you've lost him?"

✳

The Viborg City bus terminal stank of gasoline. The heartening smell of travel and distances. Behind the bullet-proof glass the saleswoman was checking his CashCard and waiting for the receipt. She was an immigrant, maybe from Samarqand itself, with deep set, black eyes and her hair hidden under a bright red scarf. He thought of Badia, her beautiful body and of her uncle's address in his pocket. He had promised to send her a postcard. Another lie. *You fucking fuck.*

The clerk handed him his ticket and CashCard.

"A single to Petersburg. There you go."

Markus thanked her. The card had worked. So far so good. In Petersburg, he would take a plane to Alexandria, then a train to Constantinople and finally another bus to Samarqand—the end of all routes, the city of evil and brutality, the perfect place for ghosts like him, those who never quite disappear because they have never quite existed. A long journey towards what? Nothingness? A new life? A certain death? An uncertain death? Check the correct answer. Only one is possible, although none might be correct.

Maybe he would meet Ole there. In the flesh or in the ghost? Would they recognize each other? Would they reminisce? Would they wave to each other and wonder?

You fuck. You fucking fuck.

He put the ticket and the CashCard in the inside pocket of his jacket and slowly walked towards the bus, surrounded by a throng of passengers.

Fellow travelers. Smiles. Conversations. Questions. Lies.

He sighed as he joined the line.

A sixteen hour trip. Perhaps he could sleep most of the way. Dream, even. Yes. *Dream.* Fortunately, he had Synth to help him do that. Something golden and warm rolled under his tongue. It tasted so sweet he had to smile.

2. THE DREAMING CHAMBeRS OF SAMARQAND

Weeping and wailing, they buried Iskander, ruler of men,
in his beloved chambers, deep in the heart of Samarqand

Al-Hussein Ben Idriss Ben Ahmed

Closing forever the gates of the Chambers, they said:
"Rest, Iskander, rest. May you continue dreaming
of your beloved Samarqand in your eternal sleep"
And they closed the doors forever and they wept.

Kalidasa

ON THE ROAD TO SAMARQAND

A flight of cranes
over a forgotten wall
- autumn wind

Chen Li

A man showed me a mound of rubble as we were leaving the city of Samarqand.
"This," he said in a disdainful tone, "is said to be the tomb of the once famed
Alexander the Great." He spat three times on the ground, which I found
rude and ill-mannered. I asked him why he had behaved in this way and he
answered it was the local custom to prevent evil spirits from coming back.

Marco Polo

THe SILENCE OF
THE STREETS

one.

Inspector-General Ali Shakr Bassam tapped on the breast pocket of his uniform, searching for the familiar cigarette pack, *Navis* without filter, red circle on a yellow background. He silently cursed between his teeth when he remembered he'd left them on the dining table of his apartment. Well, he had an excuse. They'd called him at four thirty in the morning. Hell, who would remember cigarettes at four thirty in the morning? He focused on the body that lay under the double cupola of torchlight.

"That's how you found him?"

"Yes, Inspector-General. Nobody touched anything."

Bassam clicked his tongue. A cigarette.

"Do you have a cigarette, sergeant?"

"Yes, Inspector-General."

A cigarette. Not his own brand (this was a blue pack with a galloping white horse), but a cigarette nonetheless. Foreign fingers. The wrong brand. *Galaz* filter. He smoked *Navis* without filter. Only the flame was neutral, familiar. It would have to do. Inhaling the filtered smoke deeply (Who needed filters? Why? Death had no filter, had it?) he knelt beside the corpse, pulling up his light khaki trousers by the crease so his round thighs would not be squeezed by the fabric.

The body lay on its stomach, shirtless, hands tied behind its back by plastic manacles. A black cloth hood had been put over the head, probably before the killing. A fat man, with a hairy back and a constellation of moles. A very white man, in black boxer shorts, shoeless, bathing in a dark pool of blood that had coagulated during the night. An *Eleni*—a Westerner. Just Inspector-General Bassam's luck. He wondered why there was no one from Bureau 23 yet, but someone would come soon enough. Was probably putting on his clothes right now, swallowing a mint to hide the whisky on his breath and sending away the prostitute through the back door. Bassam shivered at his thought. He really hoped no one at the Bureau 23 was capable of telepathy. He had enough trouble as it was.

"Turn him over," Bassam said. "Wait! You've got the gloves on? What? So put the gloves on, *then* turn him over."

The two policemen, two idiots from the North, peasants with flat faces, smiled sheepishly as they put on their government issue lubricated latex gloves. Bassam sighed and blew out smoke, scanning the street for clues. It was too dark to see anything. A narrow backstreet in the old city. Perfect. Extremist territory. Of course! Of course. One of the two cops, the thin one smelling of old sweat, lifted the cloth hood and rapidly turned his face away, heaving.

"Yes, yes, of course," Bassam mumbled, horrified in spite of himself.

The throat had been cut so savagely that you could see the spine through the blackening gash. The head was at a weird angle, only held by skin, muscle and a little bone; the scraggy brown beard was matted with blood.

There was an envelope taped to the man's chest.

142

Bassam was about to remove it when he caught the heavy smell of rose water and felt a presence behind him.

"Let me do that, Inspector-General."

Bassam took a step back, saluting his cousin with a sharp bow of the head and a hand swiftly brought to his heart, as if he was dusting his jacket.

Sekmet Bassam, of course. Who else? The inspector-general had known this was going to be a bad day when his cell phone had beeped in the darkness and he slammed his foot against the dining table while reaching for the tiny blinking blue screen. Which was next to his cigarettes, he remembered perfectly now—with a pang of regret. He glanced sideways at his rose-smelling cousin, hoping he wasn't a telepath. There had been stories about secret experiments. . .

Sekmet Bassam put on the latex gloves and produced a switch-blade from his pocket. His fine features were flattened by the torchlight, giving him a 1930s Fu Manchu film profile, especially with that thin, drooping mustache.

Ali Bassam hated that mustache with a vengeance.

He looked again at his cousin, who was busy opening the envelope. As a kid he had always been jealous of Sekmet's ease and handsomeness. Maybe the Enlightened had given him beauty because it had denied his family wealth, contrary to Ali Bassam's own?

The Bassam clan had a long history of family feuding. Jealousy had flourished across generations, infecting both the family and its neighbors. The most recent and dramatic event was when his great-uncle, Rusan Terbadjian Bassam, was shot by his niece while taking a bath in the family tub. At the trial she had claimed he'd raped her, but in Ali's family, everybody knew it was her father who'd given her the gun, because he coveted an olive orchard near Guldur, the hometown and cursed cradle of the Bassam clan. She was acquitted, although Ali's grandfather had tried to bribe the judge to get her sentenced to death.

"But the power of money is nothing compared to the power of pussy," his father used to say after dinner, between two puffs of his hookah and after he'd discreetly checked that his wife was out of earshot.

As Sekmet Bassam scanned the contents of the envelope Ali threw a tentative glance at his cousin, but Sekmet took out a transparent evidence bag into which he put both the envelope and its contents.

"Thank you cousin," Sekmet Bassam said. "You can go home now. I shall take care of this mess. I'll send you a copy of the letter as soon as it has been processed by the laboratory"

Ali bowed his head and retreated silently to his car. In a way, he was glad the dead Westerner wasn't his problem any more. Yet, his policeman's instinct had been awakened and he wanted the truth to be found. He felt like a good hunting-dog beaten to the fowl by a younger, faster, but less experienced male.

He opened the door of his battered Diamant and sat behind the wheel. He saw the reflection of the ambulance lights flicker against the Medina walls. It glowed red like the extremity of a cigarette. Bassam clicked his tongue a couple of times in his dry mouth.

two.

Inspector-General Ali Shakr Bassam crashed as silently as possible next to the warm, sleeping, snowy hills of Rezida. He tried to pull the sheet over his shoulder, but it was stuck under her body. He pulled harder and she moaned.

"What time is it?"

"I don't know," he whispered. "Late. Early. Too early. Sleep."

"Why did they call?"

"Murder. In the old city. Sleep now."

She mumbled something he didn't understand, then lightly snored again. Bassam closed his eyes, but myriads of blue, red and golden fireflies danced under his eyelids. A dead *Eleni*. Trouble. Of course, it *had* to be Sekmet. Was it on purpose? Things had worsened since the king had given more power to Bureau 23 because of the international situation. But why? How could the Bureau help in these difficult times? And why did he always ask himself pointless questions when he should be sleeping?

three.

The night had been short—working at Tsentsen's, then cleaning up the place, then drinking a few beers with Tsentsen, Garash and Iakov—it was becoming a routine, but it sure beat working for the Man in Viborg City. . . Markus had slept a dreamless sleep and had awoken when the sun blazed through a hole in the old curtains, prying his eyelids open like a blunt knife rapes an oyster shell.

He had some difficulty remembering his name as he sat up on the thick mattress that was lying on the blood-red tile floor. Nothing unusual, but memory glitches tended to send him into a panic. . . After all, he had stopped taking Synth almost seven months ago and yet he could still feel it rattling through his veins—Dr. Sojo had warned him: "It's a new drug. No one knows what the secondary effects can be."

Finally, his name came back to him as he reached under the mattress for his passport, secured by fifty kilos of packed straw packed in a dark blue cloth that could never be washed. When Tsentsen rented the apartment above his café to Markus, he told him that if he ever wanted to change the sheets, he'd have to rip the whole thing apart and sew on a new cover. Yeah right. Markus had decided he could put up with the stains.

He made himself some chai, eating chunks of buttered bread from a loaf he'd bought the previous day. Once he finished eating, he stood up, tea-glass in hand, opened the kitchen window and looked at the street below.

The old city street stretched both east and west, before twisting away at both ends. The apartment was on the second floor, but there weren't many buildings higher than this in the district. In the distance, you could see the proud skyscrapers of the new city reflecting the sky and the surrounding mountains as silvery cubist cinema screens.

The street was already crowded, shops were opening, traffic was building up—small cars, mostly red and blue, some white, radios turned on full-blast, were buzzing and honking, while scooters, motorcycles and bicycles zigzagged dangerously among them.

Markus closed the window, locking away the smell of spices and gasoline, and took a sip from his scalding chai.

The loud knocking on the door startled him and he almost dropped his glass on the kitchen's ochre tiled floor. He mechanically looked at his watch on the wooden table and wondered who could be coming to visit him at eight thirty in the morning. The cops, probably. Markus had already been interviewed more than ten times at the local police station since his arrival four months ago, and twice at Secret Service headquarters. Polite interviews every time, in something approximating English—they knew a lot about him, it seemed, and then again, of course, they didn't. Markus had carefully designed his new identity in Old Constantinople, from his date of birth to his political views and former jobs. He had even created a circle of friends—all fictitious, of course—who could testify for him via email. It had cost him some extra money to have these fake addresses monitored by Akmet "the Crescent"

Ozgül, his contact in OC, but you never knew when you might need them. Like now, maybe.

The door shook again under the insistent blows and Markus went to unlock it. Synth rumbled in the back of his brain, but he quieted it down. Hallucinations could wait.

"*Polisia!* Open, please!"

Markus opened the door and stared at the two men standing there. They were shorter than him, the tops of their caps just level with his eyes. One of them looked Mongolian, with a thin black pencil dab of a mustache decorating the corners of his upper lip. The other was more Turkish looking, with sweet eyes and a tired mouth. No mustache, but his cheeks were blue with stubble. They looked more annoyed in their ill-fitting uniforms than threatening—a nice change from their clean-cut, social-liberal fascist colleagues in Viborg City. They both wore a huge gun holster over the crotch area, but they held their hands behind their backs, like good schoolboys. Markus sidestepped to let them in, but they remained where they were.

"Sandorf Mathias?"

Markus still had to get used to his new alias, especially when it was said last name first.

"Yes?"

"Sorry to wake you up so early, sir. This is an emergency."

They spoke in English. That was politeness. He wondered what the prisons were like. Synth glimmered. He shut it off.

"You must come. Very sorry, sir."

Markus nodded. On the table, the chai had already lost a couple of degrees. In thirty minutes, it would be cold.

four.

Markus squeezed his meter eighty-five into the back of the small police car, cramped on a leather seat smelling of sweat. This was one of the first things he'd noticed when arriving in Samarqand: small police cars, of an unknown make, that he later identified through conversations and negative comments, as *Diamant*. Small yes, very, compared to the luxurious police limousines of Viborg City. And dirty. That was the second thing. The dirt. Not in the streets, nor in the shops. But on the cars. That dust. Mountain dust. Rocks ground to sand after a zillion years. History of history. Unknown, yet visible.

Unknown, yet visible. I like that.

Startled, Markus turned his head towards the empty space next to him. *Who said that? Who had spoken?* A woman's voice. Not Synth's. Synth had no voice. It had only provided images. Until now?

"Cigarette?"

"What?"

The hand shook the pack under his nose. Clean fingers, smelling of tobacco.

"Yes, thank you."

Men sharing cigarettes. The illusion of friendship. The small interior was soon filled with acrid blue smoke.

"Where are we going?"

The Turkish-looking policeman next to the driver turned his head towards Markus.

"The hospital. Inspector-General Ali Bassam is waiting for you there."

Markus nodded, although he had no idea why he should meet an inspector-general at the hospital.

five.

"There you go," the Turkish-looking policeman said, letting Markus be the first to walk into the cold corridor lit by evenly spaced, blinding neon tubes. A highway in reverse. Walking on a flat sky. Synth flashed for a second—album cover, music video—but he quieted it. The hospital basement was hallucination enough in itself.

six.

Inspector-General Ali Shakr Bassam looked with irritation at his watch. *What were those idiots doing?* He grunted and shrugged, pacing under the bored eyes of the second sergeant who escorted him. The sergeant was filing his nails, his back resting against the cold, white-tiled wall. Shakr knew he was a Gallaoui, and that clean nails were important to him, as they were a symbol of purity. *Whatever,* the inspector-general thought, as he absent-mindedly caressed his beard.

He was angry at corporals Nobal and Konchev, because they were wasting his time in an already perfectly pointless situation. He knew the confrontation would bring nothing, that the *Eleni* would not know this man and that the whole thing would be a forgotten episode stacked in his own memory among thousands of other forgotten episodes of the same kind. What's more, he was getting hungry.

"What the hell are they doing? Having lunch together at the city's expense?" he said out loud, to relieve some of the tension.

"I think I can hear them" the Gallaoui sergeant said, without stopping his nail-filing.

seven.

Markus' first thought was: *torture.*

At the end of the corridor—a thick double door with small opaque windows and the stench of detergent. Visions of blood hosed down a small drain in one corner, white tiles, a wooden chair.

He turned around and saw his two escorts patiently waiting for him to enter.

Torture.

But why?

Maybe they had handed his file over to the Secret Police, maybe they had found out his true identity, past, loves, hopes, dreams. That door suggested a lot of maybes. All the maybes of his life. Flashes of Synth ran along the small of Markus' back. He had never experienced Synth under duress. Stress, yes. All the time. It had been the essential reason he had become hooked in Viborg City. Easy escape. Mind in the clouds, a pure blue sky, low music humming in the background. Illusions to fight other illusions. The ghost of freedom against the ghost of oppression. "The demon you see in front of your eyes is only a projection of yourself"—*Tibetan Book of the Dead*, page something. His back pages.

He pushed the door open with his right hand.

"Enter and accept your sentence." Kafka. *The Trial.* Page—?

eight.

Inspector-General Ali Shakr Bassam turned his head at the sound of the door opening. *Finally,* he thought. *That imbecile Gallaoui was right.*

A tall, thin man walked in, longish blonde hair, morning stubble, worried blue eyes, white t-shirt with some writing on it—presumably music or some fashionable brand—black pants, no socks in the low worn-out sneakers—hurry? habit?—nice face, maybe slightly naive, although the wrinkles at the corner of the eyes and the side of the mouth denoted experience—stress? drugs? politics?—not politics, Bureau 23 would have taken care of him a long time ago—but no tourist either, he worked here, Bassam had read the reports—at Tsentsen's, a nice place, he had never been there but his son liked it—fresh fruit juice and 100 various imported beers—a mystery this young man, a mystery—and not only that—his name.

"Ah, Mr. Sandorf. . . I always wanted to know what a hero from Jules Verne would look like. . . Forgot your tiger?"

The surprise in the eyes of the young man was genuine, years of experience told him that.

"What, you didn't know? Your parents never told you?"

The young man shook his head—what, 30, 35? Maybe younger and too much experience—Were his parents idiots? Was *he* an idiot? Faking?

"I saw the TV series first, when I was young," the inspector-general resumed. "Loved it. Then later, at the police school, I found an English translation. Fabulous adventure novel. If you want, I can lend it to you sometime."

Make him feel comfortable. Good cop. No need to be bad yet. If ever. Instant sympathy. The name, probably.

nine.

That cop had taken Markus completely by surprise. The name. His name. *His fake name.* Markus mentally cursed Akmet back in New Constantinople. Did he know? Was it some kind of private joke or a random name chosen by some mischievous computer? Too late now, anyway. He managed to pull out a thin smile and shake his head.

"No, didn't know I had a famous name, nor that my parents had pulled a joke on me."

"Ah, parents. . ." the inspector-general sighed, with an amused glint in the eye. "No children yet?"

Markus shook his head.

"No."

"Parents. . ." he repeated, obviously amused by his own remark.

He was quite a large middle-aged man, with a broad mustache greased the local way, and thick black hair combed back in a shiny helmet. His cheeks were adorned with a thin trimmed beard, adding to the virile impression. He looked somewhat Persian, with half-open eyes that always seemed on the brink of closing, but with the pupils black and alert. His uniform was impeccable, as if he wanted to single-handedly contradict the Samarqand police reputation for sloppy uniforms, yet he appeared in no way strict or militaristic.

A faint smell of citrus and subtle spices drifted pleasantly to Markus' nose, indicating pride in his appearance. Markus, on the other hand, stank of sweaty sleep—he hadn't showered yet and he wondered what the inspector-general must think of him.

"I'm sorry you've had to come here in such a way," the policeman said, in almost accentless English, "but we have a very serious matter on our hands I hope you can help us with."

"Of course," Markus replied, not knowing what the other meant.

The man motioned Markus to follow him to the other end of the large barren room, where another policeman stood, filing his nails. Markus noticed a gurney with a shape covered by a sheet. A dead body. A serious matter, indeed, especially if he was a suspect. Synth began to morph the surroundings into an old *Mission Impossible* set, but he switched it off, again. He wanted to live this nightmare with open eyes.

The inspector-general stood beside the gurney, looking grave.

"Are you ready?" he asked Markus, who nodded.

"Here we go," the inspector-general said and carefully lifted the sheet with a gesture of humanity and respect.

"I will not pull the sheet lower. The wound is quite nasty," he explained, running his index finger across his throat. "Even some of my men were shocked."

Markus nodded again and reluctantly looked at the large, bald and bearded face. A white man, an *Eleni*, as they were called here. Now he understood why they had fetched him.

"Do you know this man?" the inspector-general asked, as if he had read Markus' mind.

Markus looked more carefully at the bleached face with its closed eyes and suddenly recognition jolted his senses.

It was his old friend, his Potemkin Crew partner-in-crime, Ole. When he was arrested after hacking into an attack-satellite during the Southeast China war, it was claimed that Ole had managed to escape to Samarqand, but Markus thought it was just a rumor planted by the government in order to link the group of hackers to the "Evil City," scheming to overthrow civilization once and for all.

Markus raised his eyes and looked squarely at the inspector-general's face. Shaking his head, he said: "No."

ten.

Inspector-General Al Shakr Bassam nodded and pulled the sheet back over the *Eleni*'s face. Or rather, as he knew since the identification earlier that morning, on Olgeÿ Tazar's face. How could he not have recognized him before? Yes, the street was dark, but. . . He felt a wave of sadness as his pulse skipped a beat. Then he wondered if he should leak the news to the press now, or wait a while. Of course, Bureau 23 would be furious if Tazar's death became public knowledge too soon. Bad press for the government, bad press in the international media, bad press for the king's sister and her fanatical friends. And especially bad press for the king himself, who could really do without this right now. Watching corporals Nobal and Konchev escort Jules Verne's hero back through the door, Shakr wiped away a tear with the base of his thumb.

eleven.

In the back of the police car, Markus tried to hide his grief. He felt as if he had become no more than a mask. The policemen dropped him off in front of Tsentsen's.

"I really like your t-shirt, sir," the Turkish-looking one said, before getting back into the car.

Markus looked down as they drove away. He'd forgotten what t-shirt he'd put on when he got up that morning. It was a white tee with a blue imprint. It read: *Freedom*®.

twelve.

Markus emptied his cold chai down the sink and put some more to boil on the gas stove. He cut a thick slice of bread from the half-loaf he had left and took some butter, cheese and olives from the small fridge. He took a plate and a knife, sat down and, as he had skipped breakfast, prepared his lunch. When the chai pan came to the boil he poured a fresh cup and added the usual three lumps of sugar. He sat down again, picked up his slice of bread and burst into tears.

thirteen.

Inspector-General Ali Shakr Bassam's desk was covered with the reports and color photographs of last night's murder. His heart was filled with sorrow, a feeling he had seldom encountered in his many years in the force. Only the murder of children had caused him grief in the past, and even then he had still managed to control his feelings, except in the worst cases. But now that the murdered *Eleni* was known to be Olgeÿ Tazar, his grief was something he had a hard time coping with.

> *In the street, a dog revels in garbage.*
> *The house is empty, no light shines.*
> *And yet, my heart fills up with joy*
> *When I look at the dark window:*
> *My loved one lived here once, and I do not see a tomb*
> *—I see a garden forever in blossom*

The quote from one of Tazar's most famous poems reinvigorated him, as it always did. He glanced at the ghostly skyline of the modern city through his dusty window. How could anyone murder a poet? How could anyone strangle a singing bird? Then he remembered the note his cousin had taken from him at the scene of the murder and felt a cold rage. What did Bureau 23 know about poetry? Possessed by anger, he slammed his closed fist onto his desk. Then, after a few seconds of angry consideration, he picked up the phone.

fourteen.

Synth had perfectly recreated the apartment, Niels Juels Gade 53, in Viborg City North. The palimpsestic past. A fragile reconstruction Markus could decide to erase in one thought. But no, he wanted to be there today, searching for beers inside his fridge. The two rooms. The circular table in the middle, with the computers and all the electronic stuff. The notebooks, the manuals, the printed sheets. And the booze, the drugs, the music. Ah, the music... That was how they had met in the first place, the infamous Potemkin Crew, Nick, Ole and him. New-Noise concerts. Faces seen once, then again and again, until friendship was proclaimed through exchanged words floating over the music. Shared drinks, the *cling!* of beer-bottles brought together in one virile movement. The nodding to the beat and the knowing half-smiles. Ole with his cap, black shirt and red tie. Nick with his bleached white hair, eerily pale blue eyes, worn leather jacket and crooked smile. He with vintage rock and roll t-shirts, patched denim jacket and destroyed jeans. Youth, was it? Yes, youth it was. Had been. Tenses mixed, as always with Synth. Youth. Politics, Passions, Poetry. The 3 Ps, as Ole used to say. And here they were, just as they used to be, sitting around the small table hidden by the electronalia and technical volumes, just as they used to, before Death had caught up with them, Nick in a neon-white prison in Viborg City and Ole here, in the golden city of Samarqand.

Markus knew Ole was an avid poetry reader, as much as Nick was a comic strip fan. But he had never known he was a writer. Until now. He also remembered the rumor that *The Potemkin Overture*, the book that had landed him here after a series of personal catastrophes, had been written by Ole. He hadn't believed it then. Now, he wasn't so sure any more.

"Hey, Ole," he said, opening the fridge and taking out three beers. "Did you write *The Potemkin Overture?*"

Ole lifted his round head from looking at the computer screen.

"Not yet," he sneered.

Synth could fuck up dialogue sometimes. Nick, sitting opposite, chuckled. Markus gave his friends a bottle each and raised his own into the air.

"'Til death do us part," he said.

They laughed and toasted.

Synth was pain. Synth was innocence. Synth was truth.

ECHoes

fifteen.

"Ministry of Internal Affairs," a young male voice said.

"Yes, I would like to speak to Captain Sekmet Bassam. I am Inspector-General Ali Shakr Bassam."

"Do you have an appointment?"

"Why would I need an appointment? I want to speak to him on the phone."

Idiot! the policeman thought. *I must have interrupted his nap.*

"You need an appointment to talk to Captain Sekmet Bassam. Sorry."

"On the phone?"

The inspector-general couldn't believe his ears.

"Yes. On the phone, also."

Maybe Sekmet had given orders to block him. A cold sweat ran down his spine. Why did he have to have a cousin in Bureau 23? Bad Karma. Real bad karma. He must have really fucked up in a former life.

"Come on. Is he there, at least?"

"Yes, he is here. In his office. Behind me."

"Could you forward my call, then? Just for a minute?"

"I am sorry, sir. You need an appointment."

Ali felt a ball of fire explode between his ears. *Calm down,* he thought. *Calm down. The conversation is probably being recorded.*

"I am the Captain's cousin and if you do not put me through this minute, you will be answering the phone on the Chinese border, do you understand me?"

"One moment, please."

Shakr Bassam had to admit the idiot had courage. His voice hadn't flinched a bit.

"Allo?"

"Sekmet, this is Ali."

There was a short silence, as if his cousin tried to remember who he might be.

"Inspector-General Ali Shakr Bassam, your cousin," he explained, just in case.

"Yes, yes, of course. What can I do for you?"

"I want to know if you found out anything new about the murder last night?"

As if he was going to tell me, Ali thought.

"No, we're working on it."

"When do I get a copy of the letter? You took it from me, remember?"

"But, Ali. . . I told you yesterday Bureau 23 would be in charge."

"I want to investigate."

Ali looked at the files piled up on his desk. They could surely wait. *The Dead won't mind.*

"Why?"

"Because Tazar was my favorite poet."

There was a very short pause.

"Mine too. And also of about three million people around here. It is a state affair."

"I want to investigate and find the cowards who have done it. What did the letter say?"

A longer silence. Bassam heard a car honk outside, followed by a chorus of other horns.

"You don't kill poets," he added. "You just don't."

"Ali, I can't do anything. It's too late now. The case is almost out of my hands. If they learn that you were at the crime scene with me, they will surely pull me out."

"But why?"

"Official orders from above. I can't tell you any more."

His cousin hung up and Ali Shakr Bassam looked stupidly at his phone for a few seconds, before slamming it down. *State affair. My ass. Poetry is not a state affair, it is an affair of the people, for the people, by the people.* Then he remembered the rumors about the telepathy experiments and added, mentally: *Joking, of course.*

sixteen.

When Markus walked down from his apartment into Tsentsen's that evening, he found the owner sitting sadly in front of two glasses of beer at the far end of the counter. The radio was on, playing a heart-wrenching melody. Garash, the manager, was emptying the dishwasher and drying a glass over the sink. Markus looked at the clock behind the counter. It was a quarter to six. He had arrived early. They weren't expected to arrive before six.

He sat down next to Tsenten and asked Garash for a Coke. The manager looked sad too, and Markus felt uneasy.

"Is something wrong?" he asked, in his heavily accented Perso-Mongol.

Tsentsen nodded.

"Haven't you heard the news?" he asked. "Or read the paper?"

Markus shook his head, toying with the soda bottle in front of him.

"Here," Garash said, handing him a folded paper.

"You know I don't read Perso-Mongol that well," Markus warned.

"It's the one for the *Elenis*."

Markus looked at the front page. It was a special issue of the English-speaking paper of Samarqand, *The Samarqand*

Gazette. A black and white portrait of a man in local costume occupied half the page. Although the picture quality wasn't great, he recognized Ole's round and jovial face, smiling at the camera, looking happy and confident. Above him, printed in large deep black letters, was the headline:

NATIONAL POET OLGEÿ TAZAR MURDERED.

"This is a terrible day," Tsentsen whispered. "I am not sure we should open the bar. There might be trouble."

He raised his head and glanced at Garash, who just shrugged.

"Angry people won't come here," Garash said. "Angry people will attack public buildings in the New Town."

"I hope you're right," Tsentsen said gloomily. "If you're wrong, you'll have to find yourself another job. Actually, we'll all have to find ourselves new jobs."

They laughed half-heartedly. Markus put down the paper. He wanted to know. He had to know.

"That man, Tazar, he was really famous?"

Tsentsen raised his eyes to the ceiling and shrugged.

"You have no idea. It's like your. . . your Shakespeare here, if Shakespeare had written poetry. The greatest. National pride."

Synth created Ole's silhouette sitting at the bar next to him, the eternal beer nursed between his hands. His black suit, black cap, red tie, making him look like an angry worker going to a May Day party. . . A new wave of sadness overwhelmed Markus, and the bitterness of salt water and seaweed filled his mouth.

"But why would anybody murder him? Was it a madman?"

"*Was it a madman?* You hear that, Garash? Pure Shakespeare. No, my friend, it wasn't a madman. If only it had been a madman. . . It's worse, much worse. It's politics."

Tsentsen looked around the empty bar with his paranoid eyes.

"The king," he resumed in a whisper, "is getting old. Too old, maybe. Who am I to judge? In any case, the Western Alliance is pushing hard to destabilize Samarqand. Because of our past support for the Chinese Confederacy, they hold a grudge against us. And they are very interested in our gas fields... The king knows that and has promised more democracy, but, of course, the first elections were rigged and some people became unhappy. Very unhappy. Then there was the international bad publicity. So there have been problems here ever since. And the Western Alliance is trying to find a pretext to strangle us for good."

"But where does Tazar fit in? He was a poet, no?"

"He was more than a poet. He was a symbol. His feet were in this city, but his head touched the stars."

Markus saw Ole's body suddenly adopt gigantic proportions within the walls of the café, lifting everything with his huge shoulders, the upstairs apartment, the roof, but destroying nothing, as if he was made of gentle, cool air.

"And he wasn't even from Samarqand," Garesh added, putting his drying cloth aside. "He was was an *Eleni*, like you."

"Really?"

Markus feigned surprise, but he heard an unconvincing tone in his voice that made him cringe. Fortunately, no one seemed to notice.

Garesh and Tsentsen nodded in unison.

"I don't know where he came from—some big city of the West, Babylon, St. Petersburg, one of those. He just showed up one day and became one of us," Garesh explained.

"More than one of us," Tsentsen interrupted. "He became our national poet, the beautiful voice of our city, Samarqand!"

They raised their glasses and Markus raised his Coke.

"To the immortal voice of poetry!" Tsentsen said, ecstatically.

"To the immortal voice of Samarqand!" Garesh added, his eyes moist with tears.

To my good old friend, crazy Ole, Markus thought, but he said nothing and took a sip of his funerary Coke as his companions sipped their beer.

seventeen.

On his way home Inspector-General Ali Shakr Bassam stopped at the newsstand at the corner of his street and bought a paper. He looked at the picture of his favorite poet and shook his head. The news-vendor noticed his gesture and nodded sadly, as he handed him his change.

Shakr was happy to see that the press had been so diligent. All the papers had run special editions. He had made his phone calls from the police station's cafeteria at ten, right after his conversation with Sekmet. If Bureau 23 wanted to put a lid on the case, well, fuck them. Fuck them totally. Poetry was truth. Poetry was invincible.

DISSONANCES

eighteen.

The man was drunk and had an annoying smile. *An Eleni,* Markus thought, *just like me.*

Oh no, not like you, precious. Many Elenis have come here and were nothing like you. . . Do not worry, you are one, child. One and only. I remember you well. I keep on remembering you, although your steps led you away a long time ago. The dust of the streets here remembers. It never forgets a single footprint. Ever.

That voice. Synth as a woman. What now? No panic. Frightened curiosity, more like it. The drunken man repeated something, with an expansive gesture of his arm.

"Sorry, what?" Markus said, trying to distinguish words from the slurring.

Of course, the background music and the loud voices of the surrounding conversations didn't help.

Music helps, sometimes. It helped you. That's why you came back. You remembered.

"'Nother round," the man said, smiling again.

"Sure!"

Markus produced four bottles of *Gengis Khan*, the local beer.

"Hey, where you from?" the fat guy asked, producing banknotes.

Markus slammed the change on the counter. The stranger didn't pick it up. At least, the tip was good.

"Where you from?" he asked again.

"Petersburg," Markus lied.

"Oh yeah? We're from New Babylon, my team and I. Like it here?"

The man waved vaguely.

Across the room, Markus saw a group of four or five people sitting around a table. *Elenis*, all of them. He shrugged.

"It's alright."

"I'm sure it is, I'm sure it is. . ." the man said, nodding as though he was actually doubting his own words. "We just arrived today and we saw some demonstrations. Near our hotel. Pretty violent too. You know what's going on?"

"A famous poet was murdered. People are pissed off."

"*Famous poet*? Never heard of him where I come from."

The man grabbed the four beers and moved away to his table.

Asshole, Markus thought, pocketing the tip. Another customer squeezed to the bar and ordered a Chinese whisky.

nineteen.

"You're not eating your dinner?"

Rezida's voice sparkled through Inspector-General Ali Shakr Bassam's consciousness like light reflected by an opening window. He winced involuntarily, as if the words had somehow blinded him.

They were eating in the little kitchen, as usual, just the two of them under the harsh light-bulb—Amir, their son, was away at university, enjoying his student life and newfound freedom. At least, that was what he was supposed to be doing, although Bassam had always secretly regretted that his son was such a *nice guy*, quiet and gentle, not so much a *nerd* in the Western TV series sense, but more the sensitive, brooding type. Amir had enjoyed reading and counting as a child and, if he didn't mind playing football in the yard with the other kids, he also liked to watch documentaries and play alone in his room. His long eyelashes attracted the girls and he was everybody's friend—the perfect son, in a way, but the inspector-general had hoped he would be somehow *wilder*. A strange desire for a policeman, he admitted, but that was the truth.

Bassam looked at the delicious fish his wife had prepared and felt his stomach grumble. Sadness had made him forget he was hungry. Olgeÿ Tazar's funeral was scheduled for tomorrow. More sadness. Riots, perhaps.

"Yes, yes, I'm eating," he said, lifting his fork.

Rezida clicked her tongue.

"Will you tell your wife what's bothering you? Twenty years we are married, I know my husband."

Bassam smiled. She *did* know him, maybe even better than he knew himself. She had a keen eye, and none of his little mannerisms escaped her notice.

"I'm thinking about Olgeÿ Tazar. I can't believe the case went to Sekmet and Bureau 23. It should be mine. And it's the funeral tomorrow. . ."

Rezida gently put her hand over his on the reddish-pink, floral plastic tablecloth. Her wedding-ring shone under the light.

"I'm afraid of riots. I understand the anger, but violence is not the solution. Not in this case," he resumed, still staring at her fingers.

"The broken window, the broken door can be replaced. . ." Rezida quoted. *"But nothing can replace my broken heart."*

Tazar's *Ode to a Broken Window.* Every citizen in Samarqand knew it, especially since Hataman had put it to music.

"I need to find the bastards who did this," Bassam said. "I owe it to this city."

"Do what you think is best," Rezida said calmly. "But don't bring down the roof of your own house. And eat your dinner."

twenty.

The group of *Elenis* were the last ones in the bar, two young guys, the drunk middle-aged idiot and a woman whose age was hard to guess, sitting at their table covered with empty *Gengis Khan* bottles, talking noisily about whatever they were talking about. Markus finished cleaning the other tables, holding empty glasses with the fingers of both hands, like a Norman Rockwell milkman. Tsentsen took the glasses from his hands and put them in the dishwashing machine.

"I'm going home. You can close when they're gone, or you can make them leave and then close."

Garesh had left earlier. It had been rather a slow night—people fearing the violence in the New City would spread to the old district. They had been wrong, but apparently no one had bothered to tell them. Like everywhere else, news channels always focused on the spectacular and left the reality out. The good thing was that Markus' Perso-Mongol was too limited to understand the garbage that went with the images.

"Hey, come here!" the idiot shouted at him. "Let us buy you a beer!"

Markus felt like declining the invitation, then thought *what the hell* and grabbed himself a *Khan*. He lifted it to toast with the group, but they waved at him to join them.

Tomorrow was Ole's funeral. A hangover could be a good thing.

He took a chair and sat next to a younger guy, who had thick black glasses, thinning blond hair and a scribbled goatee.

The idiot raised his bottle.

"Cheers, friend. What is your name?"

"Mathias," Markus answered, without asking their names.

"We're here on an historical mission," the idiot resumed. "You might have seen us on TV. The show is called *Archeology Action*."

The other three nodded, staring at Markus intensely with booze-soaked eyes.

"Oh yeah?" Markus carefully answered. "I don't have a TV."

They stared at each other in disbelief. The woman shrugged. She had a thin featured face, black eyes, no makeup, longish black hair and a long, thin mouth that didn't smile a lot. Her eyes glowed softly once in a while, hinting at the possibility of great beauty. They reminded Markus of tiny obsidian Aztec mirrors.

"I have the show on DVD somewhere. I'll bring it to you next time. Anyway, you know why we're here?"

Markus shook his head.

"Try to guess," the idiot taunted him.

"I don't know. . . black ops?"

He saw the smile on the idiot's face freeze for a split second and then his eyes refocused, making Markus wonder if he was really so drunk after all.

"Black ops! You hear that, guys?"

They laughed in unison. It sounded genuine.

"That's what they thought at the Embassy too, and at customs. . . They kept us hours at the airport. . . We're still waiting for some of our gear," the other guy—same age as the one with glasses, but with dark hair parted on the left and bluish cheeks eaten by acne—said.

The older idiot shook his head and rested his *Khan* on the table.

"No, try again."

"No idea!"

Markus didn't feel like playing. He was tired and longed for his bed. His soul felt like melted rubber. He could almost smell it too.

"Alexander," the idiot said, eyes shining.

"Alexander?"

The idiot nodded.

"Alexander the Great. His tomb. We think we might have found it. Finally."

"Congratulations."

Markus raised his bottle again and they all enthusiastically followed suit. The idiot went on explaining that Alexander's tomb had never been found. He'd died in Babylon, been buried in Alexandria, and then, around 400 AD, his tomb had completely disappeared. But the idiot had traced it through newly discovered Chinese, Mongol, Persian and Indian documents. . . It was here, somewhere.

"We heard of a complex of ancient caves, in the mountains. Man-made, supposedly. As soon as our gear is cleared, we're on it. Wish us good luck."

Markus wished them all the luck in the world and told them he was closing.

twenty one.

The music from the Indian-built portable stereo flowed softly in the darkness. Eyes open, staring at the omega gray ceiling, eyes open, thinking, Markus. Puzzles, chunks of huge icebergs drifting on a dark sea, lights reflected in a rainy train window, blurred collisions, Mathias.

Yes?

Who am I?

Can you reformulate the question?

Who am I?

That is the same question.

To live is to be coinciding exactly in time and space. Perfect coordinates. Synth created a diagram. He was X. He was living. That was clear enough. But for what purpose? As Camus put it, Sisyphus was happy pushing his rock up the hill because it gave him a purpose and a meaning to his rebellion.

Why am I here?

To hide.

And...?

Can you reformulate the question?

What am I here for?

To live.

What do you mean by "to live"?

Static. The sound of a nail scratching skin.

What do you mean by "to live"?

Synth created a blinding sun and the smell of warm stones. Markus adjusted the light and took in the smell, he warmed to the elements of nature.

The question remained unanswered.

twenty two.

On television:

A thick crowd, clad in white, follows a dirty-white pick-up truck. A body wrapped in white linen lies in the back. The crowd is chanting funeral songs. Some women are beating their chests, men are either shouting, singing or crying silently. The streets of old Samarqand are filled with this white cloth snake, inching its way past the closed shops. A reporter comments on the scene, while the cameras zoom in on the security forces escorting the funeral procession. One man is standing out in the whiteness, although his hair is blond. He is an *Eleni* and he is dressed in black. But no one seems to notice.

THe sOUNd OF ONe HANd CLApPING

twenty three.

On television:

Tazar's widow was interviewed at her home by the national channel. Ali Shakr Bassam stopped adjusting his tie in front of the large flat screen. Of course, the widow. Maybe she knew something. She probably knew something. He mentally registered her name—Faiza Tazar. A serious looking young woman in traditional Perso-Mongol clothes, dark circles under her eyes suggesting sorrow—but her deep black eyes showed anger. Cold anger. Behind her, a color photograph of the Poet, on a shelf, a white scarf placed over it. He would go and talk to her. Sekmet would be mad if he learned about that—perhaps he would even threaten him. It was highly illegal to work on a case that was in the hands of Bureau 23. But a Poet had been killed, and when one was working on the death of a Poet, rules didn't apply any more. Ali Shakr Bassam shut down the TV, went into the kitchen to kiss his wife and closed the door of his flat behind him. A new day's work awaited him—a new day of uncertainty and revengeful rage.

twenty four.

The girl was waiting at the bus stop. As in any cheap sentimental novel, Markus' heart skipped a beat. Although the feeling wasn't new—his heart had skipped a beat for many girls before—the precise familiarity of the feeling made him feel awkward—out of place, to be precise. It made his surroundings suddenly appear more exotic than they used to be—or rather it brought back their exoticism in a second—an impression that had faded after months of living here. The colors seemed brighter, the smells more pungent, the sounds more deafening, his freedom more vulnerable, the words more... ah, the words... The words, they were actually. . . gone. Not only his poor Perso-Mongol vocabulary, but *everything* had been wiped out for a fraction of a second. A tiny electric shock and his brain had completely disconnected his language functions. Synth graciously offered him a dictionary, but Markus shrugged it off. He liked the feeling of the *tabula rasa*. The bus arrived. The girl climbed in. He followed her, speechless, but not eyeless.

twenty five.

The only free seat was right in front of her. Of course.

Of course. It cannot be otherwise. The things you provoke, you provoke them into existence.

The woman's voice replaced his inner voice. Her words covered his words, alien and beautiful as gold and diamonds inserted in teeth.

It cannot be otherwise.

twenty six.

The bus was going downtown, in the New City. She sat before him, looking through the large dusty window. The girl. The girl from so many songs he had heard before. Yeah, *that* girl. He didn't know if he should discreetly stare at her, or glance at her reflection in the window. Beautiful. As beautiful as the streets of Old Samarqand passing by, yellow and white, all prepped-up and full of vital, polluted, noisy energy. The girl pressed her forehead against the window—her hair was cut in a page-boy style, with a fringe that stopped right above her eyebrows, she had long arched eyelashes, perfect almond-shaped, melancholic black eyes. She was half-smiling, though, like a Mongolian Mona Lisa. Mystery of mystery. The bus stopped and started. Stopped and started. At every stop he expected her to leave, but no, she was still here as the urban landscape changed, transitional chaos of the slums with children running around, always children running around, and then the New City, tall, powerful, clad in its steel and smoked glass armor. Markus felt a twinge of angst. He was getting off at the next stop. He stood up. She remained seated. *That* girl.

twenty seven.

The building where Tazar had lived was one of those large, gray social constructions bordering the Old Town like a fortress wall. A tangible border. They had been built more than thirty years ago and now had a strange charm, like a premature ruin. The train tracks zipped through them like an open scar. Olgeÿ had many times been offered a better place to live, but he loved it here. He said it reminded him of Viborg City and why he had hated it so much. It kept his poetry alive, he said.

Inspector-General Ali Shakr Bassam scanned the surroundings to make sure there were no Bureau 23 agents keeping watch. He watched a local train rumble in the distance and spotted a group of young men in tracksuits and Western-style caps, who were obviously the local hoodlums. Maybe he would talk to them later on. Maybe they would know something.

He walked towards the entrance of the monolithic structure and looked at the names on the postboxes. Fifth floor. He pushed the elevator button, but nothing happened. Of course. He had known that all along. Sixth sense.

Sighing, he started to climb the cold concrete stairs. He stopped on the third floor, and wiped some sweat off his forehead with the back of his hand.

"The bird is lighter than air but heavier than the soul."

Quoting Tazar always gave him strength and he continued his grunting ascent until he reached the fifth floor. It was the last door on the right.

He looked for a doorbell, but there wasn't one so he knocked as delicately as he could. He heard the light shuffle of feet and the turning of a lock. The door half-opened and a young woman's face appeared.

"Hello, I'm Inspector-General Ali Shakr Bassam."

"Yes?"

"I'm sorry to bother you, but I have some questions to ask you."

The deep brown eyes looked at him with obvious distrust.

"But the police have already been here. Bureau 23."

By the way she pronounced it she obviously didn't approve of the Bureau.

"I know. Here is my badge, but. . . Well, this is not really an official visit. . ."

Tazar's widow—*a woman too young and too beautiful to be a widow,* Ali Shakr Bassam thought—looked surprised now, holding onto the half-opened door of the apartment.

"Wait," he added.

The inspector-general extracted a thin book from the inside pocket of his jacket.

"Look," he said.

Hands slightly trembling, he opened Tazar's collection, *The Yellow Window* and showed her the inscribed front page: *To Ali Shakr Bassam, sincerely, Olgeÿ Tazar.*

"You see? I'm a fan of your husband. . . Uh, of Tazar. . ."

The widow nodded briefly.

"Come in," she said. "That idiot from Bureau 23 had never read any of his stuff."

twenty eight.

Every time Markus walked into the *Imperial Bookstore*, as it was called, he felt uplifted. The smell of ink and paper. The piles of books, the colors, the people—yes. The *people*. Crowded. The bookstore was always crowded. All ages. There were six stories in the store. Six. He remembered the *bookstores* in Viborg-City. The neons. The hip coldness. The plug-in book-vending terminals where you could download the books you had just bought. Bestsellers. Only bestsellers. And the classics, of course. If you wanted anything else, you either had to find it on illegal sites or buy old, yellowed paper copies. Synth recreated Carlo's shop, but Markus blocked it. There was no need for that here. The *Imperial* was great. Nothing to be replaced or morphed here. He suddenly realized that since his arrival, he was getting more and more annoyed with Synth. The pills had dried up a long time ago, on the way here. He still remembered the anguished night in Ur, waiting for the withdrawal symptoms. But nothing happened. Only more Synth creations, without the need of any pills. It felt as if Synth was a part of him now. Or he a part of Synth. He couldn't forget what Dr. Sojo once told him, about Synth being a genetically engineered drug. DNA poison. Good name for a band. He smiled in spite of himself and decided to take the elevator to the sixth floor, where all the foreign books were. Synth looked at him with half-closed eyes, vexed and frustrated.

twenty nine.

So here he was, in Olgeÿ Tazar's famous apartment. Faiza Tazar ahead of him him in the narrow corridor leading to a small sitting room, all walls lined with bookshelves. Here and there, an empty space was filled by a painting, an etching, a drawing. A huge portrait of Tazar hung over the sofa on which Faiza sat. Shakr looked at the image of Tazar admiringly while lowering himself into an old armchair.

"A friend of his painted it? It's truly amazing. So lifelike. . ."

"I painted it," Faiza answered coolly. "Now, you said this wasn't really an official visit. . . What is it, then?"

Ali Shakr Bassam cleared his throat and ran a hand through his shiny black hair.

"As I've told you, I am a. . . was. . . am a fan of his. His poetry touched the deepest parts of my soul and. . . I was called to the crime scene. I was the first officer there and I. . . I examined the body. . . Your husband's body. . ."

Shakr felt a terrible sadness come over him as he spoke and he had to clear his throat in order to carry on.

"I was supposed to be in charge of the investigation but. . . My cousin. . . Well, Bureau 23 took the case. As you know."

The young woman nodded slowly. He saw that her look had changed. It was more intense, more focused now. Feeling

THE SONG OF SYNTH

encouraged, he resumed, wiping his hands with an invisible cloth.

"I still want to investigate. On my own. I am afraid Bureau 23 wants to bury the case under official secrecy. But Tazar cannot be buried, be forgotten in such a way. He has to remain alive, in all of us. He is our voice. Still."

The widow smiled at him for the first time.

"What you say is very beautiful, Inspector-General. But I am afraid you will only get in trouble. Tazar knew he was threatened. He didn't care. He taught me not to care either. Death is only a door."

Ali Shakr Bassam felt a slight flutter of irritation.

"You don't want to know who killed your husband?"

Faiza shrugged slightly.

"The murderers are not the ones who used the knife. You know that."

The inspector-general nodded.

"Of course. But still. I believe in justice, as incredible as it may seem. Do you have any idea who it could have been?"

The young woman looked away, frowning as she thought about his question.

"A lot of people hated Tazar, for a lot of different reasons. The Fundamentalists, because of his take on official religion. The Royalists, because of his defense of freedom. The Progressists, because of his faith. . . Other poets, jealous of his talent."

Shakr Bassam smiled at the irony.

"No idea, then? Really?"

Faiza sighed.

195

"Look at the political situation. We're on the brink of war—either civil or global, or both. The Western Alliance is pressing us with all its might, the United Cities of the South are mocking our democratic attempts, our only support is the Chinese Empire, whom everybody else hates. Who cares about a poet? Who cares about music at a time like this?"

"I do," the inspector-general said. "With all my heart. Don't you?"

Faiza smiled again, but this time it was a shy, almost imperceptible smile.

"With all my heart too. But the *heart is the weakest spot of the body*," she added, quoting her husband.

"*But the strongest spot of the soul*," he said, finishing the stanza.

Faiza stood up and held out her hand. He gently took it, her fingers were soft and warm

"You two should have met," she said. "He would have liked you very much I think."

thirty.

The local hoodlums were still hanging around by the building next door. Four young guys, dressed in Western fashion. *Western television style*, Shakr Bassam thought. He had never been to the West, but he didn't believe that people dressed like they did in music videos.

They watched him as he hurried towards them, and by their slightly frightened eyes he judged them *inexperienced*. They probably sold small quantities of hashish and stored stolen goods, but hadn't entered the *real* crime world yet. He wasn't sure they even really wanted to, although they tried to look tough. Sometimes these kids made excellent cops.

"You stay here all day?" the inspector-general asked the young man who seemed to be the alpha-male—gold chain around the neck, expensive sunglasses, fancy haircut and standing up while the others sat on the concrete steps leading to the building's hallway.

"Why do you ask?" the boy answered defiantly. "You the police or something?"

The others laughed, looking at him provocatively. They reminded him of his son at 15. But they must have been in their early twenties. Without saying a word, he took out his wallet and showed them his badge. The laughter stopped at once and their eyes darted in all directions. *Really small fry*, he thought.

"You knew Olgeÿ Tazar?"

"Yes, yes, of course," the *leader* said, much to Bassam's surprise. "He was very respected around here. A great man."

He even put a hand on his heart, a gesture imitated by his goons.

The inspector-general nodded, slightly moved by the respect shown to his favorite poet by these young punks. They had slightly risen in his esteem.

"Well, I am trying to find out who killed him."

The four young men slowly nodded in unison, waiting for him to continue.

"You have no idea, I guess?"

They all shook their heads. *Of course.*

"In any case, I would like you to help me."

They waited, motionless, their eyes watching intently like soldiers waiting for their officer to order them to charge the enemy. He extracted a card from his wallet and handed it to the leader.

"If you see anybody unusual going into the Tazars' building, let me know. If you hear anything concerning Tazar's murder, let me know, ok? If you help me. I'll find a way to make it up to you, I promise."

The leader nodded, and showed the card to the others. As he made his way back to the car, the inspector-general felt extremely moved, and he was glad that his back was turned to the young men. People respected poets here. People respected poetry. No, he was wrong—it was more than that: people respected people.

thirty one.

"Excuse me, do you know anything about Wilhelm Reich?"

The voice was timid, almost accentless. Markus turned around. The girl from the bus stood before him, two books in her hands. The girl from the bus. Of course.

Of course. Accidents are the common rule.

Her eyes were smiling under the fringe. Markus put back the science-fiction novel he had been glancing at.

"I'm sorry to bother you, but you're the only. . . uh, *Eleni*, here, so I thought I might ask you. . ."

She had said the word *Eleni* with that caution people used when using a word that had derogatory undertones. But she'd smiled at the same time.

"Wilhelm Reich?" he repeated, trying to muster evasive memories from his student days in Viborg City University.

"Yes."

The girl looked at the books she was holding.

"I'm doing research. Not on him directly, but on some of his stuff. . . I wanted to know which one was the most interesting. Do you know?"

Markus took the books from her and felt the warmth of her fingers. That girl.

He read the titles. *The Orgone Energy Accumulator, Its Scientific and Medical Use* and *Selected Writings: An Introduction to Orgonomy.*

Shaking his head, he gave the books back to her.

"Sorry, I really don't know. I guess it depends what you're looking for."

She shrugged and smiled back.

"I don't really know. Yet. I'm doing some research and I came across his name. Do you know it's the last case of official book burning in the West?"

That girl.

thirty two.

He'd ordered a chai and she some Western coffee. Of course.
Of course.

They were sitting in the café located on the top floor of the bookstore, a comfortable room with low sofas and soft leather pouffes. A Géricault setting.

He had invited her and she had accepted with an amused smile. *Accidents. The common rule.* His thoughts escaped him now. He let them escape.

Her name was Saran, she was 29 and a medical researcher at the university's hospital.

"And you?"

Markus shrugged.

"I used to be in IT. Now I'm working at a bar in the Old City. Tsentsen's. Maybe you know it?"

She shook her head.

"No, where is it?"

She took a pen from the breast pocket of her embroidered suede jacket and opened the book she had just bought—*The Orgone Energy Accumulator*—to the last page, so he could write the address down.

"And your name?"

He suddenly realized he hadn't given her that vital information and they both laughed, she covering her mouth as if it was obscene to show tongue and teeth.

"Thomas."

Names are shields or weapons. You have chosen wisely, my beautiful.

Something warm rolled in his throat as he pronounced his real name for the first time since he had left Viborg City. No—not left. Escaped from. The words had to be put back in place now. Synth materialized a dictionary. Thomas decided to ignore it.

"Thomas," she repeated. "It's a nice name. Very... Western."

They laughed again.

He felt naked in front of her.

He felt completely vulnerable.

He felt completely complete.

Not Markus. Not Mathias.

Thomas.

Thomas.

thirty three.

On the bus, on the way back, another name jumped into his memory. *Badia.* He had lost the paper with her uncle's address on his way to Samarqand. He thought of sending her a postcard, but he didn't remember her address. And—trying to survive as a NoCred immigrant in the heartless Northern city—she had probably forgotten him anyway.

fLUtes ANd SKiN-dRumS

thirty four.

Routine is another way to reconcile past and present, putting the future on hold. Routine, routine, routine. Wiping up the last table at Tsentsen's was routine. It felt good.

Ole had been buried a week ago, the riots and violence had subsided, business was good again and from what he could understand with his limited Perso-Mongol, the political situation, although still tense, had regained its familiar complexion. Tsentsen and Garash could argue again, like they used to. Sometimes Synth would produce Ole's massive silhouette at the bar, drinking *Khans* all by himself, with his familiar sardonic half-smile. Thomas would secretly wave to him once in a while and Ole would slightly raise his bottle, with a sharp bow of the head. Good old Ole. Ever so dramatic. Even in death.

Thomas—he couldn't think of himself as Markus or Mathias any more—these names were the reflecting shields for the strange reality he was living in—Siamese twins that didn't even exist, even if Synth once in a while would unexpectedly produce a beautiful tiger at his feet—finished his job and slowly walked back to the bar. Tsentsen and Garash were engaged in a chess game, as they often were when they guessed the evening would start slowly. It was a Tuesday. They were probably guessing right.

As if to prove that logical reasoning is always faulty, the door opened and a small, loudly chatting group entered.

Oh no, Thomas thought. *Not them.*

The *Elenis* searching for the tomb of Alexander the Great sat down at a table, and looked around, as if they were discovering the place for the first time. Thomas wearily walked towards them.

"You just opened or is it a bad day?" the older guy said, with a grin. "Mathias, right?"

Thomas nodded. Names. Just names.

The Eleni put out a large hand with fat fingers. Thomas grabbed it reluctantly. It was strangely callous—maybe they were archeologists, after all.

"Richard. And this is Mark."

He pointed at the younger dude with the thinning hair and the glasses.

"Todd."

The other guy with short brown hair and a bad dose of acne nodded.

"And Sylvia."

The woman stared at him, expressionless.

"Four *Khans*, right?" Thomas said, desperately wanting them to go away as fast as possible.

Richard nodded and looked around, to see if any of them wanted something different. When Thomas came back with the beers on a tray, the *Eleni* paid with a crisp new banknote.

"Any chance you can take a two-three days or so off your job?" he asked as Thomas was giving him back his change. "Good money. Interesting job."

Good job. Interesting money. Think about it, not-Markus. Ah, the dreams, the dreams... Lessons to be learned.

Thomas was about to shake his head, when the woman's voice resumed.

All expeditions fail. You know that first-hand, no, not-Mathias? Why not? Adventure? You were always looking for adventure. Things happen in no particular order. Tricky, tricky. But adventure, not-Markus. . . Adventure...

"You speak Perso-Mongol, right?"

Richard was looking intensely at him now, eyes shining, as if he was secretly begging.

"Some."

"Enough to get by, I see. You work here. It's not particularly a tourist place. . . We only found it because our hotel is nearby... Cheap as dirt, and just as clean. . ."

They quietly sneered in unison.

Your name will always remain a secret. But I know it. I have always known it.

"I don't know if I can," Thomas said. "When would it be?"

"We're leaving in three days," Richard said. "Good money. And maybe a little bit of fame, even."

They always say that. Even you. That's what you told your friends, remember?

Thomas nodded and walked back towards the bar, where Tsentsen and Garesh were still playing their game. Garesh had more pieces on the board and Tsentsen looked upset, chewing his lower lip and shaking his head.

A little adventure couldn't hurt, could it? A change of scenery for a few days? What's more, he hadn't seen Saran again. She hadn't come by and he was feeling disappointed. Cheated. Sad? Sad. So leaving for a few days could help, maybe. Synth dressed him up in French Foreign Legion uniform and he couldn't suppress a smile. Adventure. . .

Ah.

Yes, that invisible woman was right, whoever she was. Adventure.

He asked Tsentsen if it was okay if he took three or four days off, with no pay. Tsentsen nodded without looking at him and moved a tower.

Remember?

thirty five.

Routine. How Inspector-General Ali Shakr Bassam used to love that word, and how much he hated it now. He grabbed the pack of Navis without filter from his desk and gently tapped it on the wooden surface to extract a cigarette. Half a dozen files were spread in front of him, all completely uninteresting. Drug dealers, failed gangsters, small time criminals. . . Routine, routine, routine.

The small-time trafficking hoodlums he had talked to near Tazar's widow's place hadn't called back. He wondered if he should find some pretext to have them brought to the station where he could interrogate them one by one. They could be accessories to the murder, in spite of their avowed respect for Tazar. Who knew? Since when could a cop trust a punk? He was getting soft. Sighing, he picked up a file. Drug smuggling. Opium. Of course. No new exotic drug or whatever. Opium. Routine. He shrugged.

MOnGOLian THROaT
ChaNT

thirty six.

Thomas got out of the Land Rover and stretched. He ached all over, but that wasn't the worst thing. His ears still rang from Richard's non-stop flow of *amusing anecdotes*. A seven hour trip. He had switched Synth on and off a couple of times, pretending to sleep, but it hadn't been enough.

He looked around. The small village was located in a breathtaking landscape, surrounded by pale yellow and ochre mountains, covered with patches of dried grass that were home to a few tiny blue and yellow flowers. The sun was setting, turning the impossibly large sky a strange blue, like ink mixed with water.

The other two Land Rovers parked behind them, in the empty main square. A small troupe of children materialized, running towards them.

The expedition could begin.

Adventure.

thirty seven.

Thomas exchanged a few words with the mayor of the village, a middle-aged Perso-Mongol with a proud, drooping, salt-and-pepper mustache. He had obviously been waiting for the expedition, as he had put his best suit on—a Chinese-cut, brownish three-piece that smelled of mothballs—and he was escorted by the local cop, a young man with a closed face who looked like a soldier from Genghis Khan's army. His cap was nonchalantly set on the back of his head, and his large leather holster hung across his thigh like a threatening S&M device. He asked to see the official papers and looked at them for a very long time, before finally nodding silently and handing them back to Richard without a smile.

"Should I give them *backsheesh*?" Richard whispered in Thomas's ear as he folded the papers back into place.

Thomas shrugged.

"I don't know. It might be insulting. Give them some cigarettes. As a friendly gesture, not as corruption."

Richard motioned to Mark, who opened the hatch of the second Land Rover and took a few cigarette cartons out. The officials accepted them with smiles and little bows. Thomas wondered what Alexander had brought them, if he had ever passed this way.

Dreams, the invisible woman's voice said. *Dreams they have never forgotten, even if it seems so. Dreams are invisible, but you can touch them. Oh, of course, you would know that. Not-Markus! You would know that.*

The mayor pointed out a large house on the other side of the square. The local inn. Thomas suddenly felt terribly thirsty. Like Alexander's horse.

thirty eight.

In his bed, Inspector-General Ali Shakr Bassam contemplated the ceiling and tried to find sleep. He imagined a starless sky hanging over him, a sky without poetry. Thoughts whirled in his head, disconnected, but they always came back to Tazar, one way or another, like black poison.

To his surprise, Amir and a few friends were organizing a tribute evening to Tazar over the weekend, and he had been invited. He still wondered if he should go—the inspector-general in the midst of all these subversive students, but he had been disappointed with the official tributes—an old interview shown on the national TV channel, a poor interpretation of one of his plays and a one minute silence at the National Assembly this morning. Bassam sighed and rolled onto his side, his back to Rezida, who moaned slightly. Although Tazar had been deemed a National Living Monument just two years ago, the renewed tension with the Western Alliance had made him less popular with the authorities. That, and the fact he advocated absolute democracy, whatever that meant. But to Bassam, all this was politics. Tazar's poetry concerned life, and life only. Yes. *His* life.

thirty nine.

Thomas had slept remarkably well, considering the narrow bed he was given, but at least, he had a tiny room of his own—right under the flat roof. The other guys had to share one big room and he was sure Richard snored like a bear. Sylvia also had a room of her own, but that was because she was a woman. He knew why he'd had the privilege—he spoke some Perso-Mongol and didn't look too thrilled at the prospect of visiting the caves.

At dinner the cop asked him what he thought of his companions. He'd answered *dumb tourists* and they laughed together, raising their half-empty bottles of *Khan*.

Thomas knew the cop would not cause them trouble, as long as the political situation demanded politeness towards the Western Alliance. There was some irony in this that didn't escape him. If he understood correctly what Richard told him in the Land-Rover, they were here to try to prove that Alexander had been re-buried here, and that would make Samarqand—symbolically at least—a historical part of the Western Alliance. Ancient kingdoms, ancient civilizations. Origins, the obsession with origins.

Cutural war of the worst kind.

Thomas sighed and stood to open the window. The village was already flattened by the sun, all yellows and grays.

Origins were dangerous, Thomas thought. He was happy to have got rid of his along the way.

forty.

"Here we are!"

Richard made a sweeping gesture with his arm as Todd filmed him. When he saw the camera, Thomas had panicked. Pretending he had a phobia of cameras, he had insisted on not being filmed and had Richard sign a hand-written paper promising that they would not film him. Attorneys always scared the shit out of these people, even in the middle of nowhere. Thomas didn't want Sørensen, watching a documentary on his B&O TV in his Viborg City apartment, suddenly recognizing him and setting Interpol on his tracks. . .

"*The legendary mountains of Samarqand, that made Alexander dream!*"

Thomas cautiously walked away and stopped a few seconds later, watching Mark and Sylvia unload crates of electronic material from one of the Land-Rovers.

The cop escorting them joined him and offered Thomas a Galaz.

"What are they babbling about?" the cop asked, putting the pack back in the breast pocket of his dusty uniform and producing a lighter.

"Alexander the Great," Thomas answered. "They think he's buried around here, somewhere."

The cop nodded, shielding the flame from the wind as he lit Thomas's cigarette, then his own.

"Ah, still dreaming about Iskander," the cop said. "Many poems were written about him. My name is Mikhail."

"Mathias Sandorf," Thomas said. "Like in the TV series!"

Mikail smiled.

"So many heroes for such a deserted place," he said, blowing a long plume of smoke.

forty one.

Inspector-General Ali Shakr Bassam never dreamed. But tonight he was dreaming—and he couldn't deny it. He was in Olgeÿ Tazar's apartment again, sitting in the same armchair, but this time it wasn't the poet's widow in font of him on the sofa, it was the *great poet* himself, smiling and pouring some chai into two small glasses.

"I am dreaming," Shakr Bassam said, astonished at seeing Olgeÿ so close, so alive.

"It's about time," the Poet replied, handing him the glass.

A MOMENT OF NEAR SILENCE

forty two.

The cave was like the fifteen or so others they had visited in the last few days. A natural hole that men had enlarged and decorated through the centuries. The sides had been carved during the Hellenistic period, with Greek columns and the characteristic acanthus flowers. Inside, centuries had passed and left their mark. Remnants of Greek, Buddhist, Islamic and Shamanic practices lay in a colorful rubble on the ground. The walls were covered in ancient graffiti and time-worn frescoes.

"Look!" Richard suddenly said. "Todd, you gotta film this!"

Todd did as he was told, turning on the camera's flashlight. Richard walked dramatically towards the end of the cave, where a gigantic painting of a Buddha with Greek features was smiling at them.

"I think we might have found it," Richard said again.

He sounded moved, and Thomas wasn't sure he was pretending.

"Here! See?"

Todd walked closer, and so did Thomas, followed by Mark, Sylvia and the cop.

"A door!"

Thomas squinted in the half-light, focusing on the trembling white circle of Todd's video camera. All he could see was a rectangular red stain between the Buddha's crossed legs. For all he knew it could be an erect penis later defaced by Muslim or Christian pilgrims.

Richard gestured to Mark, who handed him a crowbar. Thomas glanced at the cop, thinking he might disapprove of the impending vandalism, but Mikhail stood motionless, like a wax sentinel. Delicately, Richard banged on the red rectangle, listening. Thomas only heard some dull *clangs!* but Richard seemed excited.

"Beautiful, beautiful" he whispered. "Mark, Sylvia, get the probing equipment!"

Thomas followed them outside, accompanied by Mikhail. They watched the others haul some heavy metallic suitcases out of the Land-Rover.

"Why are they so excited?" Mikhail asked him, looking for his cigarettes.

"They think they might have found Alexan. . . Iskander's tomb."

"Ah."

He smiled.

"Grown men chasing ghosts. And they say we're primitive."

He shook his head and Thomas smiled in his turn, accepting a cigarette.

forty three.

There were a lot of people gathered at the university's auditorium. Hataman was scheduled to sing a few of his interpretations of Tazar's poems at the end of the evening, and Inspector-General Ali Shakr Bassam thought it probably was the reason for such a crowd. Although he was dressed as a civilian and had nothing to do with the notorious Bureau 23, he felt nervous in his suit. He chose a seat next to a fire exit, just in case, and tried to spot his son among the people who were busy on the stage.

He finally saw him, holding a couple of microphones which he distributed on the oversize coffee-table, surrounded by ten uncomfortable looking white chairs, that occupied the center of the stage.

Amir's eyes floated over the crowd and Bassam shyly waved at him, not wanting to embarrass his son. Amir saw him and waved enthusiastically back. Bassam felt his cheeks blush. So much innocence in that boy, it was almost a crime.

forty four.

"I see something," Richard whispered excitedly, as Todd's camera recorded everything. "Look—there, in the center of the screen. . . It looks like a sarcophagus!"

Thomas looked at the four *Elenis* bent over their machines. For the first time since his arrival in Samarqand, he felt close to Olgeÿ Tazar. So close, his eyes began to burn with both sadness and hatred.

forty five.

The evening had been wonderful, and Inspector-General Ali Shakr Bassam discreetly wiped away a tear with the base of his thumb as the ceiling lights were turned on again. He had a lump in his throat and his knees felt wobbly as he stood up among the parting crowd.

Hataman's songs had pierced his heart, and all those readings, discussions and remembrances around the great poet had been fantastic. He was, for once—he had to admit—very, very proud of his son. And of his son's friends too, of course. But especially of his son. His love for Tazar had acquired a superior form now, as it had suddenly become the cement that had been lacking between father and son.

Too moved to speak, he wanted to escape discreetly, to protect his son from the embarrassment of having to present his father the cop to his friends, but he heard Amir's voice calling him. He turned and saw Amir on the stage, waving for Shakr to join him. There was a woman standing next to him and he immediately recognized Faiza Tazar, Olgeÿ's widow.

"You can be proud of your son, dear Inspector-General," she said, extending a warm hand, which he shook quickly.

"You know each other?" Amir asked, surprised.

Faiza smiled.

"Yes. We met at one of Olgeÿ's readings, a long time ago."

Bassam nodded, accepting the lie as a wonderful present. Amir threw an arm over his father's shoulder. It was the first time he'd ever done that. The miracle of poetry.

TrAFfic NOiSE

forty six.

"Where have you been? I came here twice, but your boss didn't know when you were going to come back. Or if you were going to come back. . . He also told me your name was Mathias, not Thomas. Sorry if I remembered it wrong. . ."

Thomas threw a glance at Tsentsen who winked back. *That girl.* She was here, right in front of him. Black eyes under a black fringe. Smiling. Saran.

"I was away on an expedition. . . Well, with some guys from New Babylon, trying to find Alexander the Great's tomb. . . They think they might have found it. . . Whatever. . . I was their interpreter. . . Not much to do, as a matter of fact, but it paid well. . . And it was a nice change. . ."

She nodded enthusiastically.

"I could take a holiday myself. So much work! *Phew!*"

She wiped imaginary sweat from her brow. They laughed. Thomas was feeling lighter than air. Synth materialized the Hindenburg.

It was difficult to hear her, because she was sitting at the bar and surrounded by the usual Saturday night crowd. Richard and his clique were packing tonight, taking the first plane back early in the morning. They had been really excited by their discovery. Thomas hoped they were wrong, that it wasn't Alexander's tomb. Dreams should remain dreams.

Isn't that so, not-Mathias, isn't that so?

Saran was talking excitedly to him, but he didn't hear her. He was back in the last cave he had visited, lying on a marble altar covered with silk cushions, listening to the most incredible music he had ever heard.

Your music, not-Markus. Soon.

"So?"

Saran was looking at him with obvious expectation.

"Sorry. . . I couldn't hear you. . . So much noise here!" he apologized, taking her empty *Khan* and putting a new one in front of her.

"Do you want to come for dinner at my place tomorrow? I think it's your free evening, right?"

Thomas nodded.

"With pleasure."

Free, right?

forty seven.

Inspector-General Ali Shakr Bassam couldn't believe it. A lead on the Tazar assassination, right under his eyes! He looked up from his desk at Konchev and Nobal, standing in front of him in their ill-fitting uniforms, like a pair of serious clowns.

"Where did you find this?"

It was a letter claiming the murder of Tazar, signed by a group calling themselves the Samsara Freedom Fighters—he had never heard of them before, but new groups of fanatics seemed to spring up almost every week. He mentally cursed the king and his absurd politics, then remembered the telepathy rumors and tried to erase his own thoughts immediately.

The letter in itself was an incredible piece of evidence, but what made it even more formidable was a partial thumb print in the upper left corner. It had been dusted and there it was, shining and perfectly visible in the early afternoon light.

"My cousin works at the *Samarqand Morning Star* and they received it yesterday," Nobal said. "He immediately contacted me because he knew, through me, you were interested in the case and because he doesn't trust, *hmmm*. . . you know who."

The allusion to Bureau 23 was clear enough.

"Is there anything we can do for him, to thank him?"

Nobal smiled sheepishly.

"I told him we would take care of his parking tickets."

The inspector-general nodded.

"No problem. Tell him it's done. Do we have an ID on the thumb?"

Konchev stepped forward, and proudly extended a piece of yellowed paper.

"We do, sir."

"We do?"

Bassam heard the surprise in his own voice. He took a glance at the paper. Drug trafficking. Racketeering. The usual profile.

He put the paper down and frowned, trying to clear his thoughts.

"We have to play it safe for now. . . If Bureau 23 learns about this, you know what it means?"

The two cops nodded at the same time. They would be demoted and fired without any benefits. Prison even, maybe, although it would be hard, even for the Bureau 23, to push their case through a trial. After all, they were only trying to find the truth, and Bureau 23 didn't seem to be in a hurry to find the murderers.

"See if you can pin something else on this joker and bring him in when you do. Then we'll see who will terrorize who. . ."

The two cops nodded again. The inspector-general smiled when they left the room, then looked for his cigarettes. Poetry was great, but, sometimes, justice was even better.

forty eight.

Sitting at the kitchen table, Thomas looked at the fake passport and the untraceable credit card which lay before him on the table, under the single light-bulb. All that was left of Viborg City—Synth included. He let his hand run through his hair and sighed.

He was going to have dinner at Saran's place tomorrow. In Viborg City, he couldn't have a relationship because of his identity. Here, he didn't have an identity anymore. Or rather, he had three.

At least, the woman's voice said. *Maybe more.*

"Who are you? You're not Synth. . ."

The voice laughed.

Oh no, I'm not poison. Not at all. Quite the contrary. I am life. Eternal life. And you're back. Eternity bites its tail. As it usually does.

Thomas wondered for the first time in his life if he wasn't really becoming insane. Maybe Synth was winning a secret war against his brain. Dr. Sojo had warned him. No one knew where it came from, or what its secondary effects were, in the long term.

War, you say. You were a warrior, once. But something else too. That's why you came here, to the Chambers. The Dreaming Chambers. To hear your own music and learn. Learn who else you were. All your other selves. Ah not-Markus, if only you knew how happy I am to see you again.

"We've met before?"

Oh yes, not-Thomas, oh yes. But you know that. You surely know that. You have always loved to tease me. And you're doing it again. Oh, not-Mathias, how I adore you!

Thomas nodded, pushing the passport aside and picking up the skeleton card. He wondered if it was still untraceable or if Karen had found a way to make it appear in her logs somehow. *Karen screaming in the bathroom.* Yeah, right. With his other hand, he felt for a lighter in his pocket. He flicked it and moved the card towards the flame. He felt like destroying it, but something stopped him. It wasn't the end of the story yet. He might have to use it again. Synth superimposed a huge 1930s "THE END" over the room. "If only," he sighed, "if only."

THe SOng OF THe BIRds

forty nine.

After her orgasm, Saran fell over him, sweaty and breathless, her small hard breasts crushing his chest. Holding her hips, he moved faster and faster until the piercing pleasure blurred her smiling face. They remained motionless for a few seconds, the tip of her fingers gently stroking his cheek. The smells prevailed in silence. Different sweats, spices, perfumes. A whole new puzzle. He kissed her hair and she lifted her head to look at him. They hadn't turned the light off and she glistened under the ceiling light of the bedroom. He wondered if he looked transparent to her.

"Thomas. . ." she whispered.

He smiled, not knowing what to answer. He caressed her chin in his turn, then traced the shape of her thin mouth with his fingers. She pretended to bite him, like a panther or small tiger.

Dinner had been wonderful—chicken with rice and spicy vegetables—and she had chosen a great Chinese wine. They had talked and talked and then suddenly they were in her bed, making love. He tried to recollect the logic of history but, of course, there was none.

A brand new puzzle, a mosaic.

He had learned she was part of a research team in the university hospital—they were working on the use of music as supportive therapy in cancer treatment, depression and detoxification.

She began kissing his lips in a slow circling motion, as if his mouth was the center of a sensuous maelstrom.

"Thomas. . ." she repeated.

He had told her part-lies, but lies all the same. That he'd worked as an IT consultant in Petersburg and got tired of it all, and had come here for personal reasons.

You didn't lie to her, not-Markus. You told lies to yourself. That's why you came here, remember? To do away with lies.

"What?" Saran asked him, surprised, abruptly stopping her kissing.

"What do you mean, *what*?" Thomas replied, suddenly frightened she might have heard the voice too.

"You just froze. Did I do something. . .?"

She was looking at him with concern in her eyes. He tried to laugh it off.

"No, no. It's me. . . I. . ."

A new mosaic. Big pieces and little pieces. Red, blue, yellow, white and black. If they fit, glue them together.

"I lied to you. . . Kind of. . ."

"You have a wife? A girlfriend?"

He shook his head. Was this the end of the journey? To give himself completely to the first woman he had slept with in a very long time? He remembered a book he had bought from Carlo in Viborg City—*Crime and Punishment*. Raskolnikov, the murderous student, couldn't live with his guilt and gave himself up. Dostoyevsky definitely had a point there.

Synth turned the room into an *isba*, with a smoking stove and furs on the bed.

"You did it again!" Saran exclaimed. "Are you s

"What?"

"You just froze again, as if you weren't here anymore. Your eyes turned. . . weird. As if you were seeing something else. . ."

Thomas opened his mouth and let his words spill onto the bed like Lego bricks escaping from a broken box. When he was finished, she looked him straight in the eyes, smiled and said "wow."

fifty.

Routine.

Inspector-General Ali Shakr Bassam looked at the crime scene with disgust. The man was sitting on the couch, his throat slit from ear to ear. The smell of blood was pungent and Bassam carefully breathed through his mouth. Nobal put on latex gloves and picked up the murder weapon, a large bread knife, painted red by the blood.

Konchev wasn't here. He had managed to make contact with the terrorist scum, and had befriended him. He was now waiting for the one false move that could entitle them to nail him down, with his sorry friends. The inspector-general had put Konchev on sick leave, so nobody would suspect anything.

Nobal carefully put the knife into an evidence bag. The victim's wife had called them in hysterics and confessed to the murder. Bassam switched the TV off. A jealousy drama. *Routine. Routine. Routine.*

fifty one.

"So you're a hero," Saran said, with no irony in her voice.

She sat up and Thomas couldn't help admiring her delicate and desirable body. *That girl.*

"And a junkie," she added, this time with a smirk.

"Neither." Thomas protested feebly, sitting up in his turn.

"You really were from the Potemkin Crew? I can't believe it."

Thomas nodded.

"Yes, with Ole. . . I mean Olgeÿ Tazar. . . And Nick. He's dead too. . ."

Saran was all excited now.

"You know that *The Potemkin Overture* is a classic here? You know that book, right, that Tazar wrote. . . Ok, he didn't sign it, but everybody knows it was him. . . Wait a second. . ."

She jumped from the bed and began looking through the books on her shelves. Thomas didn't know if he should begin to panic now or if he should wait a little more. Before he could decide, she was back on the bed with a thin paperback. Although he couldn't read the cover, he understood immediately what it was.

"I have to read it again," she said. "You're in it!"

Thomas nodded nervously.

"Don't tell anyone, OK? No one! If Viborg City or the Western Alliance learns I'm here, I'm dead!"

She put the book between her knees and stared at him for a few moments, looking very serious.

"Can't you go to the authorities? I'm sure they would treat you like a hero. . . Look at Tazar. . . Well, he never officially said who he was, but I'm sure they knew. . ."

"He was just murdered. I wouldn't be surprised if it was a dirty trick from Viborg City or the Western Alliance. And the authorities couldn't protect him."

She nodded sadly, put the book aside and cuddled up in his arms. Her warmth and weight made him feel safe again.

"I'm afraid it might be some of our own. The political situation is very complex nowadays and Tazar made a lot of enemies with his poetry. . . But you're right. Maybe you shouldn't tell anyone. . . Can I call you Mathias then?"

"No!"

He'd almost screamed.

Not-Markus. Not-Mathias. Not-Thomas?

"Call me Thomas, please. But maybe Mathias in front of others," he added, carefully.

Saran nodded and remained silent for a few minutes. He could hear her breathing.

"You know, I know Tazar's widow, Faiza? She was my art teacher in high-school. We have kept vaguely in touch. I think you should go and visit her."

Thomas remembered her from the funeral. A dignified woman with a beautifully tragic face.

"I don't know. . ."

"You were a friend of her husband. A close friend. . . If it was me, I'm sure I'd love to hear some anecdotes about my late husband. . ."

Synth began to rumble and flashes of the old apartment in Niels Juels Gade began to be superimposed over his eyes.

"You're OK? You're switching off again. . ."

Thomas nodded, but his smile was crooked.

"You're right," he said. "I am a junkie."

DODECAPHONY

fifty two.

They hadn't slept much, and Thomas found the suburb of Samarqand where Ole had lived the last and happiest part of his life quite depressing under the late morning sun. The only spot of color in the large concrete blocks, which weren't so different to the ones of Viborg City—and that might have been why Ole had chosen to live here—was the blue dome of the Bibi-Khanym mosque he could see in the distance.

Saran had called Faiza Tazar earlier in the morning, right after breakfast, and she had immediately agreed to meet him. "See?" Saran had said, sitting on his naked lap and kissing him with triumphant strength.

A few people hung around here and there, by the entrances, like any other suburb of the world, the young wearing Western outfits and smoking pot, the older guys discussing international politics, the state of their marriage and the fate of their children.

Saran pulled him by the hand and they entered a building, suddenly absorbed by the piss-smelling shadow.

fifty three.

As he climbed the stairs—the elevator was out of order, of course—Thomas reflected about the situation, as his mind slowly emerged from the shell-shock of sleep. Was everything happening terribly fast or, on the contrary, was he still living his life in slow-motion, events deformed by their own dynamics and history by its own entropy? He looked at Saran's back walking up the stairs in front of him. Karen? Not-Karen? Who was she? He didn't even ask himself that. The essential question. A cold trickle of sweat rolled down his back. Who was waiting for him in the apartment? Sørensen? He stopped for a second, his heart beating inside his throat. Saran disappeared at the top of the stairs.

He suddenly felt like running away. Synth morphed the stairs into escalators in a huge train station. He was about to turn on his heels when Saran's voice stopped him.

"She's waiting for us," she simply said.

Magical words.

fifty four.

Faiza Tazar held him for a long time, her hands grasping his arms with emotion.

"Olgeÿ talked about you so many times I feel I know you. It's wonderful to see you, so wonderful. . . He would have been so happy. . . But sit, sit!"

A lump in his throat, Thomas sat next to Saran under a huge painting of his friend in traditional Perso-Mongol clothes. Faiza sat down in a large leather armchair, and poured chai into three glasses.

"He would have been so happy to see you," she resumed, lifting the glass to her lips and blowing gently over the surface. "He was so proud of you. . . Have you read his book?"

Thomas nodded, although he didn't want to explain under what circumstances. Ole would have undoubtedly been much less proud of him. . .

Politics, not-Markus. Always politics. They're an evil wind one must follow.

"Please, tell me your story. . . How you came here. . ."

As a legendary bard, leaving the annoying pieces out, Thomas told her most of his story, stressing all the parts that featured Ole. When he was finished, he realized that Faiza was silently crying, two discreet silvery lines glimmering down her cheeks.

She held out a hand, which he grasped.

"You know he wrote beautiful poetry. . ." she said, almost gasping. "A lot of it was inspired by his experience with you."

Thomas nodded, not knowing what to say. He felt Saran shift position on the sofa, pressing herself softly against him.

"And I'm sure a lot was inspired by you, too" he finally said, recovering his voice. "Much better poems than the ones I inspired, no doubt."

She smiled and wiped her tears with both hands.

"I have something for you."

She got up and disappeared into a small study. Saran quickly kissed him on the lips and winked.

"There," Faiza said, coming back and giving him a book.

Thomas couldn't read the title, printed in elaborate Perso-Mongol calligraphy.

"It's called *The Traveler's Songs*, and it's dedicated to you. . . See. . ."

She gently made him open the collection on the first page. Something was written. His name, in Perso-Mongol.

The gift is always given at the end of the journey, not Mathias. The story is eternal.

He was about to thank her when someone violently banged on the door.

"Police! Open up!"

They looked at each other with surprise, and Thomas saw fear flicker in the women's eyes. Gesturing them to remain seated, Faiza went to open the door.

fifty five.

Inspector-General Ali Shakr Bassam mentally thanked his lucky star. He had been right to trust those local hoodlums. They had called him as soon as a stranger had appeared to contact Tazar's widow. An *Eleni*. Of course, the man could be anybody—a friend, a tourist, a journalist. But who knew? He might also have been connected with something bigger, much bigger than themselves, that had to do with Tazar's murder. When he turned his hand into a fist to bang on the door, it was the fist of vengeance. No, better than that—it was the fist of justice.

fifty six.

Inspector-General Ali Shakr Bassam looked at Thomas with unconcealed surprise. What was the hero of a Jules Verne novel and of a bad TV series doing here? And where was his tiger?

"Thomas, this is Inspector-General Bassam."

Thomas nodded and stood up, extending a hand. Somewhat stunned, the policeman shook it rapidly.

"Yes, we've met," the *Eleni* said.

"Indeed," Bassam said, recovering his martial air. "But your name wasn't Thomas, if I recall correctly."

The *Eleni*'s face blanched.

This is too easy, the policeman thought, *whatever is going on here. The guy is an amateur. The Western Alliance is probably suffering from budget cuts again.*

"I have something to explain," the *Eleni* (*Thomas* now) said.

The young woman who was sitting next to Thomas stood and took his hand.

How long had they known each other? What did she really know about him? And what was Faiza's role in all of this?

"My real name is Thomas Wesenberg. I was part of the Potemkin Crew. I want to ask for political asylum."

Inspector-General Ali Shakr Bassam opened his mouth, then closed it slowly. Why did it always have to fall on him?

FREe JazZ

fifty seven.

In the back of the little Diamant, Thomas re-lived various episodes of his life, in broken sequences. Saran sat next to him, talking to the inspector-general who was behind the wheel. They were talking too fast for him to understand, but it didn't matter. He felt relieved and scared at the same time—open gates, closed gates?

Ah, not-Markus, not-Mathias, can any gate be otherwise? Timing is essential and I am your time now. I am entirely yours.

In spite of himself, Thomas smiled at his own reflection in the window. It didn't smile back.

fifty eight.

Ali Shakr Bassam hated Bureau 23 headquarters with all his heart. Although he was nothing of a revolutionary, he resented secret services from all over the world, including his own city. Things had to be done in the open. That was the best guarantee for a regime. If only the king could understand that... He tried to cover his thoughts as he talked to the security officer who had stopped them in the huge, impeccable, gray marble hall.

The man nodded like a robot and escorted them to an elevator. The inspector-general noticed the surveillance cameras following them as they walked. He felt like making a discreet obscene gesture, but he wasn't a kid any more and he had an important mission to fulfill.

fifty nine.

"Come in."

Sekmet's office was even larger than Bassam had imagined and he suddenly wondered what his actual rank was in the Bureau's hierarchy. He quickly kissed his cousin on both cheeks, in the traditional fashion and the smell of his expensive Western cologne tickled his nostrils. Sekmet was dressed in an impeccable pigeon-gray suit, that fell perfectly in place whatever gesture he made.

He also shook Thomas's hand, but told Saran she had to wait in the antechamber, where two security officers were sitting, at opposite sides of the room.

Bassam noticed the look of distress in Thomas's eyes as the door closed behind her, but Sekmet flashed a reassuring smile, as he motioned him to a seat in front of his desk. Bassam sat next to him, crossing his legs to look more imposing.

"Thank you, dear cousin, for contacting me about Mr. Wesenberg. I appreciate this very much."

To Bassam's surprise, Sekmet sounded genuinely grateful. *He must have taken acting lessons*, he thought. *Or he has a hidden agenda.* Strangely, both possibilities seemed equally credible.

"Before we get to the paperwork, Mr. Wesenberg," Sekmet said as he sat down himself, "I have to tell you that it is a great honor to meet you. As you know, the Potemkin Crew is quite a legend in our parts. Not to mention South-East China, of course."

He smiled, but it was impossible to read his thoughts. Bassam suddenly hoped he had done the right thing by contacting him.

"We have a problem, however."

There we go, Bassam thought.

Sekmet stood up again, and walked towards a window overlooking the modern city.

"As you know, our diplomatic relations with the Western Alliance are strained, to say the least. We are desperately trying to buy some time, even peace—at any cost, it seems."

The inspector-general glanced quickly at Thomas, who understandably seemed ill at ease.

"I am sure," Sekmet resumed, not looking at them, "that some of us would even think that handing you to the Viborg City authorities would do wonders for our reputation with the Western alliance. . ."

The inspector-general felt his heart gallop in his chest. He had brought this young man, this hero, Tazar's best friend, directly into the mouth of the crocodile. Sekmet turned his glance towards Thomas and smiled again.

"Let me reassure you immediately, Mr. Wesenberg. I am not one of them. But I have to hide you from them too. So I cannot make a public announcement of your defection. All I can do, is to give you a new identity, working papers and a monthly sum of money, until you can fend for yourself. Does that sound reasonable to you?"

No medal, no TV interview, no meeting with the king, Bassam thought. *Fuck them.*

Thomas nodded.

"You also will have to sign a paper stating that you will not partake in hostile actions that can endanger this city's security."

The *Eleni* nodded again.

"That means no hacking," Sekmet added, letting his eyes linger on the *Eleni*'s face.

Sekmet took a pile of papers on his desk and pushed them towards Thomas, who began to leaf through them. Handing him a pen, the Secret Service officer lifted a finger, as if he had forgotten something. He opened a drawer in his desk and took out a small red box.

"It is my duty and my honor," he said, slowly opening the box, "to give you this medal on behalf of the king and the city of Samarqand."

Bassam looked at the Golden Crescent and gaped. The highest military distinction. It wasn't so bad after all. They had recognized his actions. He wondered if Tazar also had had one. He would ask Faiza about it, if they ever met again.

Thomas accepted the medal with a weak *thank you* and began signing the papers. Sekmet leaned back in his chair and winked at Bassam. The inspector-general winked back. He couldn't wait to get out of here.

sixty.

Saran stood up as Thomas walked through the door. He opened his arms and hugged her for a long time. Inspector-General Ali Shakr Bassam was almost moved to tears. He wondered what kind of poem Tazar would have written about that. Sekmet grabbed him gently by the arm, preventing him from leaving the room.

"We have to talk, cousin," he said, "but not here."

Bassam felt his blood freeze inside his veins.

sixty one.

In the unmarked car taking them back to Saran's apartment, Thomas explained what had happened. She patted his hand, and said nothing. Her eyes were as deep as a starry night under her silky fringe and he realized that he loved her. *That girl*. It was as simple as that. He had only come to Samarqand to meet her. All the rest was literature, as a French poet had once said.

sixty two.

They had driven for more than an hour, until they reached the edge of the desert. The mountains in the distance were bluer than the sky.

What now? Inspector-General Bassam thought as he exited the unmarked car. *A bullet in the back of my head, like in the good old times?*

Sekmet got out in his turn, putting on very dark sunglasses. He took his jacket off and his white shirt almost blinded the policeman.

"Ali," Sekmet began, leaning against the car and lighting a cigarette without offering one to his cousin. "We have to talk. Seriously. That's why we're here, where no one can hear us."

Bassam nodded, looking for his own *Navis* in the pocket of his shirt.

"You have to drop your investigation into the Samsara Freedom Fighters."

"What?"

How did he know? Bassam felt his knees grow weak. The end of his career. The disgrace. How could he ever face Rezida again? And Amir?

"We know you're onto them. Konchev contacted us and he's working for us now. It was too big for him to handle. I understand."

A blinding white rage flashed in Bassam's eyes. The bastard!

"It's a trap, Ali. A beautifully designed booby-trap. We knew it was them all along. We also know that they are funded by the Western Alliance's secret service, through various cover organizations. They're linked with the Democratic Front—not officially, of course. But they are. You know what that means, don't you?"

The inspector-general reluctantly shook his head. He hated to be mistaken for an imbecile. Especially by his own cousin.

"If we hit on the Samsara assholes, the Democratic Front will say we're attacking democracy and what not. Perfect excuse for the Western Alliance to tighten its grip on us, and provoke a war or worse, a civil war. You understand now?"

Bassam nodded slowly.

"So what are you going to do? Let them kill more people?"

Sekmet looked away, puffing on his cigarette.

"Some people will die, yes. It's the sad truth. But we're trying to prove that the Democratic Front is linked with the Samsara assholes. Your man is helping us with that. He's either extremely courageous, or completely stupid, I'm not sure which."

Bassam had no doubt. The second adjective was the right one.

"But what if they unmask him?"

"It's a risk. We have other options too, don't worry."

"So they will never be punished?"

Sekmet threw his cigarette way.

"Who knows? Maybe there is justice in this world. Or in the next."

His smile was sardonic and, for a fraction of a second, Bassam saw him as a human being.

"And what about me?" Bassam finally said, after a long pause. "Am I under arrest for disobeying a direct order? Or demoted? Fired?"

He laughed nervously. Sekmet opened the door of the car and looked for something in the inner pocket of his jacket.

"Here," he said, handing Bassam a white, unmarked envelope.

My death sentence, the policeman thought, but he didn't care any more. He had heard too much already and the few illusions he still had had been blown away farther in the desert.

He took the letter out and unfolded it. He frowned and read it again.

"Promoted? To inspector-general first class? But why?"

He didn't know if he should feel proud or insulted.

"You know why, Ali," Sekmet said, patting him on the shoulder and opening the passenger door for him. "You're anything but an imbecile."

As he bent over to take his seat, Bassam had to admit, to his great despair, that his cousin was right. On both counts.

sixty three.

"Now that you are officially a hero," Saran said as they sat on her sofa to relax after the day's emotional turmoil, "we have to treat your drug problem."

THE dREamiNG ChAmbeRS Of saMarqaND

sixty four.

She had explained everything to him and yet he was scared. It had been two weeks of morning visits to the university hospital, a modern white building that was surprisingly beautiful. He actually felt comfortable there, but then again, dating one of the lead researchers probably helped too.

They had taken blood samples, DNA samples, whatnot samples—always smiling, always talking, explaining to him what they were going to do with them. The weirdest thing was when they had asked him to write down the fifty songs he loved the most.

In the evening, coming back after work to meet Saran at her apartment, they would discuss what was going on. The tests had shown that Synth was indeed a DNA drug— probably manufactured by the military. So Dr. Sojo had been right all along. Normally, there would be no cure and the most likely prognosis was a permanent psychosis. The mysterious woman's voice was a good example of that. Fortunately, Saran and her team had been researching new types of therapy. It was lucky he had met her, and yet what was luck? As the woman inside him would have said.

And here he was today, lying on a stretcher in a circular white room, feet and ankles bound by thick leather straps as a drip slowly seeped its miraculous cure into his veins. Saran walked in, coming into his field of vision. She was wearing her doctor's uniform and held a large pair of earphones, which she put over his head.

"You OK, darling?"

Thomas nodded as best he could.

"This is still experimental," she said, caressing his forehead and kissing his mouth with closed lips. "I really hope it'll work."

She kissed him again, harder this time. Thomas tried to relax as the lights dimmed in the room and a strange music began to fill his ears. He didn't know if it was the drip, the music or a combination of the two, but he began to feel wonderfully relaxed and deeply, deeply, happy.

It seemed that the music revealed his inner joy, a joy he had forgotten, if he had ever felt it before. The sun appeared in the corner of an open window, a small bird flew like an arrow across the garden and the smell of cherries filled his nose.

He felt exhilarated and couldn't stop smiling, it was as if he had smoked the biggest joint on earth. But he wasn't feeling groggy, not at all. Quite the contrary, as a matter of fact. He felt one hundred percent lucid and totally in control. Rhythms and melodies he had never heard before, but that were still familiar enough for him to feel safe and relaxed intertwined in his brain. Saran's smile and the curve of her armpit. Ole's laughter. Nick's bad jokes. A walk on Viborg City's main street in the summer. Saran's smile and the curve of her hip. He closed his eyes in the reddish half-light. Something like gold and honey was running through his veins—he could almost picture its luminous path.

Suddenly, he felt a presence next to him. He opened his eyes again. It was a woman. Saran? He tried to focus, but her face was blurred, like an object moving too fast for a camera.

263

So you came back to the Chamber, loved one.

He recognized the voice, but he wasn't frightened any more.

They are playing your music, I hear. Soon, you will be cured and we will have to part.

"Are you Synth?" Thomas asked, surprised. His mouth felt like he had eaten eaten too much chocolate, heavy and sweet.

The woman's laughter had a crystalline quality that blended with the music, like ice cubes in water.

No, not-Markus, not-Mathias, not at all. I am part of this music. I am your calling, your melody. And soon, I'll have to blend to let you free, just like I did before.

"I don't understand. Who do you think I am? I have never seen you before."

Ah, but Iskander, you have. In your dreams, you have. That's why you came back to me, Iskander. To fulfill your dream once again.

"I am not Iskander."

Oh, you are, not-Thomas. Here, you are. You are in my Dreaming Chambers. You are back. And I can prove it. What is your deepest dream, not-Thomas?

Thomas tried to concentrate, but his mind kept following the uninterrupted melodies chasing each other behind his eyes, like smoke from different cigarettes.

"I want. . . I want to topple empires."

The woman laughed again. It was the most beautiful laughter he had ever heard.

See? What did I tell you? Goodbye, not-Thomas. Goodbye.

"Wait!"

He tried to raise his head as the figure seemed to be absorbed into its surroundings.

THE SONG OF SYNTH

"Who are you?"

Laughter again. This time, far away.

I have many, many names, not-Markus. But you can call me Samarqand.

The last word sounded like a tiny flute note, exploding like a soap bubble as it ebbed and died. The room suddenly morphed into a cave and he was standing naked and free at its center.

He realized, without ever having been there, that he was on the other side of the red door that Richard and his team had discovered in the last cave. The cave was dimly lit, like the room in the hospital, but there was no distinguishable source of light. He recognized the familiar red rectangle and another painting of the Buddha, in much better shape than the one outside the door. Nearby there was what looked like a marble altar. Walking closer to it, Thomas saw that it was an empty sculpted bed. He touched the stone with one hand. It was surprisingly warm. Lifting his head, he noticed a silhouette and he knew it was Synth.

It had the shape of a man. Thomas took a careful step towards the ghostly apparition, and saw that it had his features. The ghost looked at him and smiled. Then sneered. Then disappeared with a terrifying howl. Without knowing why, Thomas howled with it.

sixty five.

When he woke up, he felt completely disoriented and it took him a few minutes to realize that he was lying in a hospital bed, in a small white room, with a monitor attached to his arm by a couple of electrodes.

He felt drained, and yet curiously, whole. He wondered if Synth had left him for good and tried some mental associations, with no effect at all. And then he realized that sanity scared him. He tried to laugh it off, but his mouth twisted in painful grimace.

The door opened and Saran's head appeared, She smiled at him and he smiled back. Looking at the monitor, she lifted his arm and took his pulse. She then took a pen-like flashlight and examined both his eyes.

"Panic is normal after treatment," she said matter-of-factly. "We haven't found a way to stop it yet. Sorry. But it'll pass, don't worry."

Thomas saw dust dancing in the sunlight and he tried to sit up. He thought it would be difficult, but he managed without any problem.

"You are still in shock," Saran explained to him. "Otherwise your body is fine. Actually, we're going to walk out of here together in a few minutes. That's the big advantage with our therapy—it's not invasive in any way."

Thomas looked at his clothes folded on the chair. Life. Waiting for him.

"That music. . . It was beautiful. What was it?" he asked, actually feeling better by the minute.

Saran had a little laughter.

"You."

Thomas looked at her, perplexed.

"The list of your favorite songs. . . I have. . . Well, we've discovered that people like music that corresponds to their biorhythms. . . If you want, moods, feelings, thoughts are all algorithms in some ways. . . So we track the patterns and come up with melodies that should fit the psyche perfectly. . . And help or trigger the curing process. . . So, you were cured by yourself. . ."

Thomas shook his head.

"I'm not sure I understand, but I'll accept that."

"I'm not sure I really understand either," Saran said, stroking his cheek, "but it seems to be working. No more Mr. Freeze, I hope."

He pulled her to him and they kissed. This time no image, no metaphor, no cinema scene interfered with the feeling of her tongue wrapping around his. That wonderful, incredible feeling of pure, untouched, untainted reality.

WIND ON WIND

sixty six.

Inspector-General First Class Ali Shakr Bassam sat looking at the various open folders spread across his new desk. His new office was much larger than the previous one, and he could see the dome of the Biby-Khanim mosque, if he leaned through the open window and let his eyes follow the avenue. Someone knocked on the door, and he told him to come in.

Nobal appeared, a file under his arm.

"What is it, sergeant?"

"The suspect has confessed, sir. I need your signature."

Bassam took the documents, skimmed through them and walked to his desk to get a pen. He initialed the papers and gave them back to Nobal, who slammed the door behind him. *Routine*, Bassam thought. *Routine. Routine. Routine.* It was a wonderful feeling.

sixty seven.

Thomas kissed Saran's cheek. She was still sleeping and he didn't try to wake her up. He would only be gone for a few days. Picking up his backpack, he left her apartment and walked down the stairs. He was supposed to meet Golovin, the chief archeologist of the mission, in front of the history department in half an hour. They were going to find the long forgotten Dreaming Chambers that had once made Samarqand famous and had attracted Alexander the Great, who believed they would cure his long-lasting depression. Thomas secretly laughed at Richard and his cronies, probably desperately trying to get a visa to come back and find Alexander's tomb. He hoped they would be watching TV when the documentary about the Dreaming Chambers' extraordinary discovery was shown.

Before hopping on the bus, he took the skeleton credit card out of his pocket and walked towards an open garbage can. Nearby, a little boy in rags was kicking a ball against a wall. Thomas had often seen him in the street and he knew he was a street urchin. He hesitated for a few seconds, holding the card above the smelly garbage-can, then dropped it.

When he climbed into the bus, he saw the kid double over the garbage-can and pick up the card. As the bus started, the kid ran in the opposite direction, almost knocking down an old woman who, raising her fist, angrily cursed him.

"Watch where you're running, Temudjin, you little bandit!"

ABOUT the AuTHOR

Seb Doubinsky is a bilingual French writer, born in Paris in 1963. An established writer in France, Doubinsky has published a series of novels covering different genres, from classical literature to dystopian fiction, as well as a few poetry collections. He currently lives in Denmark, with his wife and his two children, where he teaches French literature, culture and history at the university of Aarhus.